D0463397

Discard

ALSO BY LIAN HEARN

LORD OF THE DARKWOOD

THE TALE OF SHIKANOKO · BOOK 3

LORD OF THE
DARKWOOD

LIAN HEARN

FARRAR, STRAUS AND GIROUX · NEW YORK

Farrar, Straus and Giroux
18 West 18th Street, New York 10011

Originally published in 2016 by Hachette Australia
Published in the United States by Farrar, Straus and Giroux
First American edition, 2016

Map by K1229 Design

Library of Congress Cataloging-in-Publication Data
Names: Hearn, Lian, author.
Title: Lord of the Darkwood / Lian Hearn.
Description: First American edition. | New York : Farrar, Straus and Giroux,
    2016. | Series: The tale of Shikanoko series ; book 3
Identifiers: LCCN 2016016694| ISBN 9780374536336 (paperback) | ISBN
    9780374715038 (ebook)
Subjects: LCSH: Japan—History—1185–1600—Fiction. | BISAC:
    FICTION / Literary. | FICTION / Fantasy / Historical. | GSAFD:
    Fantasy fiction. | Adventure fiction. | Historical fiction.
Classification: LCC PR9619.3.H3725 L67 2016 | DDC 823/.914—dc23
LC record available at https://lccn.loc.gov/2016016694

Designed by Jonathan D. Lippincott

Our books may be purchased in bulk for promotional, educational, or
business use. Please contact your local bookseller or the Macmillan
Corporate and Premium Sales Department at 1-800-221-7945, extension
5442, or by e-mail at MacmillanSpecialMarkets@macmillan.com.

www.fsgbooks.com • www.fsgoriginals.com
www.twitter.com/fsgbooks • www.facebook.com/fsgbooks

10 9 8 7 6 5 4 3 2 1

Might it be through grief
at sight of the bush clover,
colored by autumn,
that the stag's cries continue
until the foothills resound?

—from *Kokin Wakashū: The First
Imperial Anthology of Japanese
Poetry*, translated by Helen Craig
McCullough

THE TALE OF SHIKANOKO
LIST OF CHARACTERS

MAIN CHARACTERS

Kumayama no Kazumaru, later known as Shikanoko or **Shika**

Nishimi no Akihime, the Autumn Princess, **Aki**

Kuromori no **Kiyoyori**, the Kuromori lord

Lady **Tama**, his wife, the Matsutani lady

Masachika, Kiyoyori's younger brother

Hina, sometimes known as Yayoi, his daughter

Tsumaru, his son

Bara or Ibara, Hina's servant

Yoshimori, also Yoshimaru, the Hidden Emperor, **Yoshi**

Takeyoshi, also Takemaru, son of Shikanoko and Akihime, **Take**

Lady **Tora**

Shisoku, the mountain sorcerer

Sesshin, an old wise man

The **Prince Abbot**
Akuzenji, King of the Mountain, a bandit
Hisoku, Lady Tama's retainer

THE MIBOSHI CLAN

Lord **Aritomo**, head of the clan, also known as the
    Minatogura lord
Yukikuni no **Takaakira**
The **Yukikuni lady**, his wife
Takauji, their son
Arinori, lord of the Aomizu area, a sea captain
Yamada Keisaku, Masachika's adoptive father
Gensaku, one of Takaakira's retinue
Yasuie, one of Masachika's men
Yasunobu, his brother

THE KAKIZUKI CLAN

Lord **Keita**, head of the clan
Hosokawa no **Masafusa**, a kinsman of Kiyoyori
Tsuneto, one of Kiyoyori's warriors
Sadaike, one of Kiyoyori's warriors
Tachiyama no **Enryo**, one of Kiyoyori's warriors
Hatsu, his wife
Kongyo, Kiyoyori's senior retainer
Haru, his wife
Chikamaru, later Motochika, **Chika**, his son
Kaze, his daughter
Hironaga, a retainer at Kuromori

Tsunesada, a retainer at Kuromori

Taro, a servant in Kiyoyori's household in Miyako

THE IMPERIAL COURT

The **Emperor**

Prince Momozono, the Crown Prince

Lady Shinmei'in, his wife, Yoshimori's mother

Daigen, his younger brother, later Emperor

Lady Natsue, Daigen's mother, sister of the Prince Abbot

Yoriie, an attendant

Nishimi no **Hidetake**, Aki's father, foster father to
    Yoshimori

Kai, his adopted daughter

AT THE TEMPLE OF RYUSONJI

Gessho, a warrior monk

Eisei, a young monk, later one of the **Burnt Twins**

AT KUMAYAMA

Shigetomo, Shikanoko's father

Sademasa, his brother, Shikanoko's uncle, now lord of
    the estate

Nobuto, one of his warriors

Tsunemasa, one of his warriors

Naganori, one of his warriors

Nagatomo, Naganori's son, Shika's childhood friend,
    later one of the **Burnt Twins**

AT NISHIMI
Lady Sadako and **Lady Masako**, Hina's teachers
Saburo, a groom

THE RIVERBANK PEOPLE
Lady Fuji, the mistress of the pleasure boats
Asagao, a musician and entertainer
Yuri, **Sen**, **Sada**, and **Teru**, young girls at the convent
Sarumaru, **Saru**, an acrobat and monkey trainer
Kinmaru and **Monmaru**, acrobats and monkey trainers

THE SPIDER TRIBE
Kiku, later Master Kikuta, Lady Tora's oldest son
Mu, her second son
Kuro, her third son
Ima, her fourth son
Ku, her fifth son
Tsunetomo, a warrior, Kiku's retainer
Shida, Mu's wife, a fox woman
Kinpoge, their daughter

Unagi, a merchant in Kitakami

SUPERNATURAL BEINGS
Tadashii, a tengu
Hidari and **Migi**, guardian spirits of Matsutani
The dragon child

Ban, a flying horse
Gen, a fake wolf
Kon and **Zen**, werehawks

HORSES
Nyorin, Akuzenji's white stallion, later Shikanoko's
Risu, a bad-tempered brown mare
Tan, their foal

WEAPONS
Jato, Snake Sword
Jinan, Second Son
Ameyumi, Rain Bow
Kodama, Echo

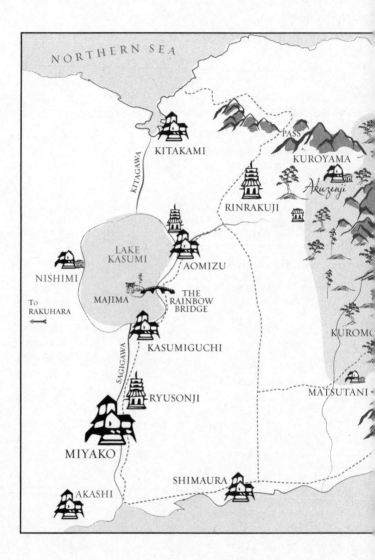

THE SNOW
COUNTRY

THE
..WOOD

Shisoku

MUENJI

KUMAYAMA

MINATOGURA

KUMAGAWA

ENCIRCLED SEA

----- ROADS

RIVERS
AND STREAMS

 CONVENT
OR TEMPLE

HUT

SHRINE

ESTATE

 TOWN

LORD OF THE
DARKWOOD

HINA (YAYOI)

The girl could see nothing. Her lungs were bursting. At any moment, she would open her mouth and breathe in the fatal waters of the lake. Snatches of her brief life came to her: her mother's face, her father's last words, her brother's cry for help before he disappeared. She had been one of the few survivors after the massacre in Miyako. Now her life was over, and she and Takemaru, the baby she clutched desperately, would join the dead. Tears formed in her eyes, only to be lost in the ebb and flow of Lake Kasumi.

Then suddenly there were dark shapes next to her, strong arms seized her. She was pulled upward toward the light, miraculously still holding the baby. She retched and coughed, gasping for air, taking great gulps of it into her lungs. Hands reached down from the side of the boat and took Take from her. He was limp and pale, but, as she herself was pulled on board, she heard him scream in ragged, outraged gasps. He was alive.

The boat bucked like a living animal in the strong westerly wind. She saw the ocher-colored sail lowered quickly, dropped on the deck, while the helmsman struggled with the oar at the stern. The men who had plunged into the water to save her were lifted up; they tore their wet clothes off and went naked, laughing. Monkeys screamed and chattered at them, dancing at the end of their cords. The sun in the east was dazzling. A crowd surrounded her. The men who were not naked were all dressed in red. They looked like beings from another world and she was afraid that she had drowned. But women stripped the heavy robes from her with hands that felt real, exclaiming at their fine quality in human voices. She and the baby were wrapped in furs, wolf and bear skins, and a bowl of some warm, strange-smelling liquid was pushed into her hands.

Men hoisted the sail again, the hemp flapping, fighting them, ropes snapping, snaking through the air. The monkeys screamed more loudly. In the confusion, one of the boys approached her, holding the lute. Beneath the howl of the wind, the slap of the waves, it was still playing, but more softly, its mother-of-pearl and gold-inlaid rosewood gleaming in the sun.

"Who are you?" he said quietly. "What are you doing with Genzo?"

Fragments of memories came to her. *It is Genzo, the Emperor's lute*, Take's mother, Akihime, the Autumn Princess, had said, and she had promised to tell her where the child Emperor was, but she had not. Could this be him standing before her? It must be, the lute revealed him. But she must hide the fact she knew who he was.

She shook her head at him, as though she did not understand, and held out her hands. His eyes narrowed as he thrust the lute at her. She saw his unease, longed to speak to reassure him, but did not dare say anything. How would she address him, for a start? Words of honor and deference rose on her tongue, but then the sailors shouted roughly at him to come and help them. Beside him the other boy was holding a text, made up of pages stitched together.

"Yoshi caught the lute and I caught this," he said, holding it out to her. "It's heavy! How did a girl like you manage to throw it so far?"

She grabbed it from him. She could not explain it, maybe it had sprouted wings and flown. She already knew the Kudzu Vine Treasure Store was enchanted. She tucked it under one arm while she turned her attention to the lute. It gave a sigh, as if it would start playing; she gripped it with her other hand.

More shouts echoed around her. The boys darted from her side and the lute quieted. It retained all its beauty, but it surrendered to her touch and allowed her to play it. It no longer played itself, in that wild irrepressible outburst of joy.

"She is a musician," one of the men who had rescued her exclaimed. "We must take her to Lady Fuji."

The other looked back toward Nishimi, now barely visible over the choppy surface of the lake. "She must be from a noble family. Someone will miss her, someone will come looking for her."

"That was Lord Hidetake's home," the oarsman called. "He is dead."

"Could this be his daughter? The one they call the Autumn Princess?"

"The Autumn Princess would be a grown woman by now," said one of the women, who had already put Take to her breast and was nursing him. "This one is still a girl. How old are you, lady?"

"I turned twelve this year," the girl replied.

"And what do they call you?"

She did not want to say her name. There came into her mind a fragment of memory, a poem. "Yayoi," she said. It meant Spring.

"Is this little man your brother?" the woman asked, stroking Take's black hair tenderly.

She knew she must not tell them that the baby was the Autumn Princess's son. "No, my mother died, a long time ago. He is the child of one of my maids." She went on, improvising, "She died giving birth to him. I like to play with him. I was holding him when I had to run away."

"What were you running from?" They were sympathetic toward her, but their curiosity was becoming tinged with anxiety.

The girl who had named herself Yayoi began to shiver, despite the furs and the warm drink.

"A bad man came," she said, and then regretted sounding so childish. "I was afraid he was going to kill me."

"We should take her back," one of the men suggested.

"Kinmaru," the other man reproved him. "Someone was going to kill her!"

"And that someone, Monmaru, could very well come looking for her and then who will get killed? Us, that's who!"

"Can't turn back against this wind," the helmsman called. "It's impossible."

❋

It was late in the afternoon by the time they came to the shore near the Rainbow Bridge. The market was almost over. Lanterns were being lit in the streets of Aomizu, on the island of Majima, and along the bridge. As soon as the boat grounded, the acrobats leaped ashore with the monkeys.

"It's not too late to do a trick or two," Kinmaru cried. Monmaru began to beat a small drum and immediately the boys threw themselves into a performance, a circle of somersaults with the monkeys, a high tower with three of the monkeys on top, a wild dance where the animals jumped from man to boy to man. A crowd soon gathered around them. Yayoi realized the audience knew the monkeys by name, calling out to them, *Shiro, Tomo, Kemuri*, and had their favorites, whom they applauded wildly. She was dazed by the noise, the colorful clothes, the shouts in a dialect she could barely understand. She gripped the lute and the text close to her chest, as though they could shield her from this strange, new world.

"Come," said the woman who had nursed Take—he was now asleep in her arms. "You will stay with us tonight and tomorrow we will ask Lady Fuji what she thinks we should do with you."

Yayoi slept restlessly on a thin mat in a room with three women and a clutch of children—one other young infant and three toddlers. The toddlers slept deeply like kittens. Take woke once screaming, and the other baby was colicky and fretful. Every time Yayoi felt herself dropping into sleep, the baby wailed and she woke in alarm, half-dreaming something had happened to Take, he had slipped from her arms underwater, he'd been stolen by monkeys. She heard the men and boys return later, their exaggerated efforts to keep quiet, their muffled laughter, the monkeys chattering as they were returned to their cages. For a few hours the house fell silent, but she thought she heard a bird call, while it was still dark, before even the roosters had woken, a long, fluting call like an echo from the past.

The women rose at dawn to prepare the morning meal. Yayoi, who had never made a meal in her life, held Take for a while. He was nearly two months old. He looked closely at her face and smiled.

He will never know his mother, she thought, and felt tears pool in her eyes. What would this day bring for them both? She felt sick and faint with fear.

"Don't cry, lady."

"Look how pale she is, white as a spirit."

"You need to be beautiful for Lady Fuji."

The women's voices echoed around her.

"Will Lady Fuji let me keep Takemaru?" she said.

They exchanged looks that she was not meant to see.

"The baby can stay with us."

"Yes, I have plenty of milk for two."

"You cannot look after him, you are still a child yourself."

"Then let me stay with you too!" Yayoi could not hold the tears in.

"This is no place for a young lady like you," Take's foster mother said.

It was cool in the early morning, but by the time Lady Fuji arrived the sun was high in the sky and the air was warm. She came in with a rustle of silk, cherry blossom petals in her hair, the sweet perfume of spring all around her.

The women immediately started to apologize on Yayoi's behalf.

"Her clothes are not yet dry."

"She's been crying, her eyes are red."

"She nearly drowned yesterday; she can't be expected to look her best."

Fuji studied Yayoi carefully, taking her head between her hands and tilting it from side to side. "I can see how she looks. What a beautiful child. Who are you, my dear, and where do you come from?"

Some instinct warned Yayoi that her former life was over and she should never speak of it. She shook her head.

"You can't tell me? Well, that may be for the best. You have a Kakizuki look to you. Are you a survivor of the massacre in the capital?"

Yayoi did not answer, but Fuji smiled as if she had acquiesced.

"Someone hid you at Nishimi, but you were discovered and that is why you ran away?"

This time Yayoi nodded.

"Can you imagine any man wanting to kill something so precious?" Fuji said. "Yet hundreds of women and children were put to death in Miyako last year when the Kakizuki warriors fled, leaving their families behind. I am of a mind to protect this one."

She looked around and saw the lute and the text. "You brought these with you? As well as the baby?" She picked up the lute and studied it with an expressionless face. It had lost its glowing rosewood and its gleaming inlay, yet Yayoi thought the older woman recognized it.

"So what am I to do with you?" Fuji said finally. "Is anyone going to come in pursuit of you?"

"I don't know," Yayoi replied. "Maybe." She held herself rigid, trying not to tremble.

"Someone must have seen you fall in the lake, but did they see you rescued? If anyone is looking for you, they will start their search with our boats, so I think I will take you somewhere you can be safely hidden. We will hold a funeral service for the children who sadly drowned."

Hina drowned and Yayoi was rescued.

"Will Take come with me?"

"How can a girl like you take care of a baby? And that would only draw unwanted attention to you. Take can stay here, the women will look after him. One more baby makes little difference to this troop of children."

She called to the women to bring some clothes, not Yayoi's own robes, which she told the women to cut up for costumes, but old castoffs that smelled of mildew and something sour like vinegar. When she was dressed, they covered her head with a cloth, which concealed her hair and most of her face.

"I must take my things," she said anxiously. "The lute and the text." Clasping them to her chest, she followed Fuji into the rear courtyard of the house, where the boys from the boat were feeding the monkeys and playing with them. A young girl was with them, idly beating a small drum, laughing at the monkeys and teasing the boys when they yawned and rubbed their eyes. Yayoi wanted to stay with them, to be one of them.

She felt the lute stir and quiver and the notes began to trickle from it. She gripped it, willing it to be silent. The girl came to Yoshi's side and took his hand protectively. Yayoi wondered if they had grown up together, if the girl was a princess like Aki.

Fuji shook her head. "It will be safer hidden away too," she said. "Kai, dear, I've told you before not to hang around here with the monkeys. Go back to your own place. I'm sure you have plenty of chores there."

"I wish I could stay here," Kai replied.

"What nonsense! Girls are never acrobats. Be thankful the musicians took you in."

Fuji helped Yayoi into the palanquin that rested on the ground outside the rear gate, the porters, two strong young men, beside it. They both bowed respectfully to Fuji, who gave them directions in a quick, low voice before she climbed in next to Yayoi and let down the bamboo blinds.

She heard the women call, "Goodbye! Goodbye! Take care of yourself."

"Goodbye, Takemaru," Yayoi whispered.

✳

The lute quieted as the men jogged and the palanquin swayed. The stuffy heat and the motion made Yayoi sleepy and she nodded off several times, dreaming in brief, lucid snatches, then jolting suddenly awake. She could see nothing outside, only had the sensation of moving from light into shade, splashing through water, then going up a steep hill, the palanquin wobbling alarmingly as the men negotiated the steps. Finally, the palanquin was set down. Fuji raised the blind and stepped out.

Yayoi followed her, glad to breathe the cool mountain air. Below her, framed by twisted pine trees, lay Lake Kasumi. She could see smoke rising from the villages around its edge and the tiny sails of boats, gleaming yellow in the sun. Behind her a bell tolled. It must be midday.

"This is a temple for women," Fuji said. "I have sent a few girls here to be looked after, until they are old enough."

Old enough for what? Yayoi wondered, her mind shying away from the answer. She concentrated on what was around her: the vermilion wooden gate, the flowering mountain cherries, the steps that led upward beneath pines that curved over them like a dark tunnel.

Fuji began to climb them swiftly. Yayoi had to trot to keep up with her. The stones were set too high for a child and, by the time they reached the top, her legs ached. Someone must have been told of their arrival, for at the top of the steps a nun was waiting to greet them. Behind her was a garden, with a spring that filled a cistern then overflowed and ran trickling away from them into a large fishpond.

"Our abbess asks that you will take some refreshment with her." She looked at Yayoi with cool, unfriendly eyes. "You have another foundling for us to look after?"

"She is called Yayoi," Fuji said. "I would prefer as few people as possible to know she is here. It will not be for long."

"No," the nun agreed, her eyes appraising Yayoi's height and age. "I suppose she can join the other girls in prayer and study." She turned and began to walk toward a low building at the side of the temple. Its roof was curved at each end in an upward swoop, like wings, as if it would take flight at any moment.

The nun paused and said to Fuji, "Asagao will want to see you. She can be this girl's friend. They are about the same age." She clapped her hands.

A girl came from the building and dropped to her knees before Fuji, who stepped forward to take her hands and lift her to her feet. She looked carefully at her, much as the nun had studied Yayoi. The girl blushed. Yayoi thought her very pretty.

"Lady Fuji," Asagao said. "I am so happy. I missed you so much."

"Sweet child, I have brought someone to be your friend. Please take care of her for me."

"Go with her to the girls' room and show her where everything is," the nun said. "Give me your things. Well, well, what have you brought with you? An old lute and an even older text? The lute will be useful, but you won't need the text here. Don't worry, we will keep it safe for you. When you leave, you may take it with you."

"Reverend Nun, may we walk a little way with you and Lady Fuji?" Asagao pleaded.

She had an enchanting manner and the nun was charmed. "Very well, since it is so long since you have seen your benefactress. Just as far as the fishpond."

Red and white carp swam peacefully in the large stone basin, beneath lotus leaves from which the flower stems were just beginning to emerge.

"See how the red and the white can live together?" Asagao said. "Why is our world so torn by war?"

Fuji smiled. "You are very poetic, my dear. I can see you have been learning well. But it is best not to speak of the red and the white. As far as the Miboshi are concerned, there are now only the white."

"Yet in this pond the white are outnumbered by the red," Asagao said, so quietly only Yayoi heard. She wondered what her story was and how she had ended up under Fuji's protection. The two older women walked on and the girls were left alone.

※

Over the next few days she was able to learn more about Asagao and the other girls. Their ages ranged from six to fourteen. The oldest was gentle, rather tall, as slender as a reed, and seemed shy and younger than her age. Her name was Yuri. The next oldest was Asagao, born the year before Yayoi. Then there were two sisters, so close in age they looked like twins, with red cheeks and a stocky plumpness that the meager food at the temple did nothing to diminish. They were ten and nine years old and were called Sada and Sen. The youngest, the six-year-old, was Teru, a thin, wiry little girl who reminded Yayoi of the monkey acrobat children. She wondered if she was of the same family and, if so, why she had been sent away to the temple.

She mentioned this to Asagao one night as they were preparing for bed. The older girls helped the younger ones, combing their hair, hanging their day clothes on the racks. Teru had fallen asleep while Yayoi was smoothing out the wrinkles from her robe. Yuri was at the far end of the room, singing quietly to Sada and Sen, who were already lying curled together. Her voice sounded thin and mournful. The plum rains had begun and everything was damp. The water fell in a steady cascade from the roofs, drowning all other sound. In the dim days, the girls became both febrile and depressed.

"Lady Fuji probably bought her from her family," Asagao said. "Many parents have no choice. Daughters fetch a good price. Everyone wants girls these days."

"Is that what happened to you?" Yayoi was ashamed of asking so directly, but could not control her curiosity.

"My mother was one of Lady Fuji's entertainers," Asagao whispered. "I am not meant to speak of it, but I want to tell you. My father was a Kakizuki warrior.

They fell in love, he bought her freedom and took her to his house in Miyako. Women on the boats don't have children—you will find out, I suppose—so I was lucky to be born at all. When the capital fell to the Miboshi, my father did not flee with the Kakizuki, but sent me to Lady Fuji, and killed my mother and himself."

"How horrible, how sad," Yayoi murmured, wondering how Asagao could still grow up so pretty and so charming.

"I think you would find all the women on the boats are the same these days," Asagao said. "They all hide tragic stories of loss and grief beneath the songs and the smiles."

She stroked Yayoi's cheek. "I am sure we will be friends."

At that moment Yayoi wanted nothing more. "Let's be friends forever," she said, seizing Asagao's hand and pressing it.

❋

The following morning Reverend Nun came into the room where the girls were practicing serving tea and other drinks, though water replaced wine, taking turns to be the male guest and the female entertainer. Playing the role of the men made the two sisters giggle uncontrollably, and Sada, in particular, proved extremely inventive in portraying drunken behavior. Asagao was equally gifted as the entertainer, distracting and calming the guests with songs and dances. They did not have to pretend to be in love with her. Even Reverend Nun watched for a few moments, her face softening. Then she recollected why she had come and said, "Yayoi, our reverend abbess wishes to see you."

This message was obviously shocking to the other girls, who all stopped what they were doing and stared openmouthed. Sada broke off in mid-sentence and began to hiccup for real. Reverend Nun gave her a disapproving look. "Perhaps this role play is becoming a little too realistic. Asagao, put away the bedding. The rest of you can do your dance practice now with Yuri. Come, Yayoi."

The cloisters that linked the buildings around the main hall were flooded and rain poured down on each side. It was exhilarating, like running through a waterfall. Yayoi found she was stamping deliberately in puddles, as if she were a little girl again, playing with her brother, Tsumaru, and Kaze and Chika, the children of Tsumaru's nurse.

"Walk properly," Reverend Nun scolded her when one unexpectedly deep puddle sent water splashing up her legs.

At the end of the cloister stood a small detached residence, not much more than a hut. On the narrow veranda a ginger cat sat with its paws tucked under it, looking morose. The hut was old and weatherbeaten; the bamboo blinds over the doorway hung crookedly and were black with mold. One of the steps was broken and there were several boards missing from the walls and shingles from the roof.

"Did you say the Abbess wanted to see me?" Yayoi said doubtfully.

"Yes—don't ask me why! She has never asked to see any of the girls before. It is most unusual."

"And she lives here?"

"Our abbess is an unworldly woman. She does not concern herself with material things. She chose this hut as her abode when she took over the headship of our community. She agreed to it only if she was permitted to live in this way, as humbly as the poorest peasant. The former abbess was very different, very different. We all miss her."

Yayoi was hoping Reverend Nun would expound more on the former abbess, who sounded interesting, but at that moment a voice called from inside.

"Send the child in."

Yayoi stepped up onto the veranda, avoiding the broken step, and pushed aside the bamboo blind. Gloomy as the day was, it was even darker inside, though one small oil lamp burned in front of a statue that Yayoi recognized, when her eyes adjusted to the dimness, as the horse-headed Kannon. A flowering branch had been placed in front of it and the sweet smell filled the room, mingling with incense, not quite concealing the whiff of dampness and mold.

"Come here. I am told your name is Yayoi." The woman stretched out a pale hand and beckoned to Yayoi to approach. Her head was shaved and her skull gleamed in the light, as if it were carved from ivory. Her features were ordinary—snub nose, wide mouth, small, rather close-set eyes—and her build, though not at all fat, was solid. She wore a simple robe, dyed a deep maroon. Her feet were tucked under her, reminding Yayoi of the cat outside.

Yayoi saw the Kudzu Vine Treasure Store, lying on a shabby cushion beside the Abbess.

The older woman followed her gaze. "You brought this with you. Can you read it?"

"I can read a little," Yayoi said. "But it often seems very difficult."

"I should say it does!" The Abbess laughed, a surprisingly merry note. "Many would call it the most difficult text in the world, if they were lucky enough to get their hands on it. Do you mind telling me how it came into your possession?"

There was something about her that made Yayoi relax, as if the woman were a relative, an old aunt or a grandmother, neither of which Yayoi had ever known. She knelt down on the cushion, moving the text aside, happy to feel its familiar touch beneath her hand.

"An old man gave it to me. I was interested in plants and healing when I was little. I used to brew up potions from dandelion, burdock roots, charcoal, and try to get the dogs and cats to drink them, when they were sick. Master . . . he, the old man, came upon me one day and asked me seriously about my ingredients and measurements and if I was keeping records of the results. Later he gave me the Kudzu Vine Treasure Store and said I would find many cures in it, but I haven't got to that bit yet." She hesitated for a moment and then said confidingly, "It only lets me read certain parts."

"Oh yes," said the Abbess. "It is a text of great power,

but I can see it would be tricky. This old man, can you tell me his name?"

"Master Sesshin," Yayoi said, and immediately wished she had not.

"Don't be afraid," the Abbess said. "Only truth is spoken in this hut. Truth is what I seek: true thought, true sight, true speech. This Master Sesshin, what kind of person was he?"

"He had a lot of books. He lived in my father's house, I don't know why, but for as long as I can remember he was there. Even when my mother was alive, before Lady Tama . . ." She recalled her stepmother's cruelty and fell silent.

"What is it that Lady Tama did?" the Abbess prompted.

"She had his eyes put out," Yayoi whispered, "and she drove him away, into the Darkwood."

"Poor man," said the Abbess. "And poor Lady Tama, who has added such darkness to her life. Was she your father's second wife?"

"My mother died when I was very young," Yayoi said. "My grandfather took Lady Tama from her husband, my uncle, and made my father marry her."

"Ah, what trouble these old men cause with their attempts to control everything! If only they could foresee the ripples that go on through generations!" The Abbess said nothing more for a few moments but took Yayoi's hand and stroked it gently.

"My husband died," she said finally. "I was still a young woman, and we had one son. I had been married at my father's command. I had not seen my husband previously. But I came to adore him, and he me, I believe. He died in the north. After his death, his brother begged me to marry him and swore he would preserve the estate for my son, but my grief was so great I could not bear to look at either of them, for they both resembled my dead husband. I chose to leave my son in his uncle's care and I renounced the binding ties of love and affection. I wanted to know the truth of this treacherous, cruel world, and why humans have to live lives filled with such deep pain."

"Did you find any answers?" Yayoi asked.

"In a way. We worship the goddess of healing and compassion here, and she has helped me. But I missed my son terribly, and when I was told he had died in the mountains my pain was no less intense than it had been for his father."

A long silence followed.

"What am I to do here?" Yayoi asked, not knowing how to respond to the Abbess's disclosures. She thought of her own uncle, her own mother and father. Why were some forced to die and others permitted to live? Where did the dead go? Did they still see all that took place on earth? How could they watch those they loved and not grieve over them and long to be with them? Why did their spirits not return more often?

"Lady Fuji has asked us to take care of you and teach you all you need to know. We do this for several girls she has sent to us. In return, she pays for the upkeep of our temple, our food, and so on. And she protects us. She has many powerful friends. There are not a few, these days, who are offended at the idea of women running their own affairs. They would like to impose a male priest to keep an eye on us. Times are changing, my dear Yayoi; even in this remote place we can sense it. The Miboshi are warriors, not swayed by gentler pursuits as the Kakizuki were."

"Can I stay here, always?" Yayoi said. She did not want to be reminded of the power struggles in the capital in which her father had died.

The Abbess said gently, "I'm afraid Lady Fuji has other plans for you. We try to give the girls skills, both physical and spiritual, so they may live the best life they can. I see you can read and write, but do you know how to calculate?"

Yayoi shook her head.

"Well, I will teach you that. And you will come to me once a week and we will read your text together."

❋

"What did she say to you?" Asagao asked jealously. "None of us has ever been sent for. What is she like?"

Yayoi had returned to the girls' room, puzzled by the conversation with the Abbess. Asagao was alone; the other girls were dancing in the exercise hall. Asagao had been told to put away the bedding, after which she was supposed to sweep the floor, but she was still lying on one of the mats, the broom abandoned at her side. Her face was flushed, her sash loosened.

"I am to learn to calculate," Yayoi replied. She did not want to speak about the Kudzu Vine Treasure Store.

"Why? Are they going to marry you to a merchant?" Asagao giggled. "You will be totting up how much rice you have sold and working out the value of the bean harvest. What a waste of a beautiful girl!"

"The Abbess will be giving me lessons herself," Yayoi said.

Asagao pouted. "You are going to be everyone's favorite. I shall be jealous. But what was the Abbess like?"

"She is rather like a cat. In fact she has a cat, a ginger one. She is merry and playful, but you feel she might scratch at any time." Yayoi looked at Asagao sprawled on the mat, saw the translucent white of her skin. "Hadn't you better hurry up? Reverend Nun will be angry if she catches you with the bedding not put away and the floor unswept."

"I have been practicing for my first time." Asagao giggled again. "I can't help myself. It's so much fun. Yuri showed me. You know she is leaving soon? Here, I'll show you. Lie down and we'll pretend I'm your merchant husband."

Yayoi's heart was beating fast, with a kind of terror. She could not put it into words, but she suddenly saw her future. She turned and ran from Asagao, ran from the room, out into the garden. Her eyes were filling with tears. She came to the top of the steps. Where would she go, if she did run away? The choices seemed stark. She could stay where she was, and hand control of her life and her body over to these others, or she could die. By this time sobs were shaking her. She crouched down, her head in her hands. She did not want to die. But she did not want to go where they intended she should either.

She heard someone behind her, and Asagao put her arms around her.

"Don't cry," the other girl soothed her. "Don't cry. I'm sorry I upset you. Our lives may be hard, but they will have pleasures, too. Maybe you are too young to understand now, but one day you will. And we will always be friends, I promise you."

They heard the Reverend Nun calling them.

"I suppose I had better finish the floor," Asagao said.

2

BARA

A little way from the capital, while they could still smell the smoke from the fires at Ryusonji, the fugitives, Shikanoko and the Burnt Twins, paused in their flight at a remote temple. Eisei insisted they bury the Autumn Princess though Nagatomo thought Shikanoko, numbed and silenced by grief, would have ridden on with her dead body until he too passed away. The temple was neglected and the monks, whom Eisei knew, were reluctant and taciturn, yet Nagatomo thought he would not mind it as a final resting place, against the side of the mountain, looking out over the narrow valley where the flooded fields reflected the bamboo groves and the clouds, and the wind sighed in the cedars. The funeral was hasty, with little ceremony. The lord, as Nagatomo called Shikanoko in his mind, stayed with the horses, watching from a distance.

Nagatomo thought someone else watched, too. In the

next few days he was aware a woman was following them. The horses knew she was there; the foal frequently turned with pricked ears and alert eyes, staring back the way they had come, until its mother called in her fretful, anxious way. The lord did not notice. He noticed nothing.

"It's just a coincidence," Eisei said, when Nagatomo mentioned her. "She is on a pilgrimage or going home to her birthplace."

"Traveling alone?" Nagatomo replied. "And who goes into the Darkwood on a pilgrimage?"

The great pilgrim routes all lay to the south. There were no sacred shrines or temples, and no villages, in the huge forest that spread all the way to the Northern Sea. Apart from the occasional hermit, no humans dwelled there, just wild animals, deer, bears, wolves, monkeys, and, it was said, tengu—mountain goblins— as well as huge magic snakes and other supernatural beings.

When they stopped to eat and sleep—though Nagatomo knew the lord did neither—the woman hid herself. She lit no fire; he wondered what she ate, who she was, what she wanted from them.

The rain had lessened to a steady drizzle, but the trees still dripped heavily and the streams and rivers spread out, drowning the path. The fake wolf jumped from rock to rock. It did not like getting wet. The horses waded through water up to their hocks. The lord rode the silver white stallion, Nyorin, and Nagatomo and Eisei doubled up on the mare, Risu, though both preferred to walk.

The mare was bad tempered and ill mannered, and bucked and bit, without provocation. The foal was still nursing and the mare stopped dead whenever it demanded the teat.

At night they removed the black silk coverings they both wore and caressed each other's ruined face. It did not matter, then, that no one else would ever look on them with desire again or understand the terror and agony as the mask seared away skin and flesh. They were the Burnt Twins. They had found each other.

Only the lord could wear the mask. Nagatomo knew it had been made for him in a secret ritual by a mountain sorcerer. Usually it was kept in a seven-layered brocade bag to be taken out when the lord walked between the worlds and talked to the dead. But now, on the journey into the Darkwood, he wore it day and night. The polished skull bone, the cinnabar lips and tongue, the antlers, one broken, the black-fringed eye sockets through which glistened the unending tears, transformed him into a different creature.

"He cannot take it off," Nagatomo whispered to Eisei.

"Cannot or will not?"

"It is fused to his face in some way."

"It must be because of what happened at Ryusonji," Eisei said, as if he had been thinking about it over and over. "The dragon child was awakened, my former master destroyed. Finding that overwhelming power, and releasing it, came at a price."

"Has it burned him?" Nagatomo wondered aloud. "As it did us?"

"He does not seem to be in pain," Eisei replied. "Not physical pain," he added, after a long pause.

Mid-afternoon on the fourth or fifth day—he was beginning to lose count; every day was the same: steep gorges, flooding rivers, huge boulders, the wild cries of kites in the day and owls at night, the humid air that made them sweat profusely until just before dawn, when they shivered in their sodden clothes—Nagatomo noticed the woman was no longer following. The foal had been restless, trotting back along the track, almost as if it were trying to attract his attention, making its mother balk and neigh piercingly after it.

The lord was far in front, Gen, the fake wolf, close to the stallion's heels, as always. Eisei pulled on the mare's bridle, yelling at her.

"I'll catch up with you," Nagatomo said, and began to walk back the way they had come. The foal whickered at him. It was uncanny how intelligent it was; often it seemed on the point of speaking in a human voice. It trotted confidently ahead of him.

He told himself he was being a fool, trailing after a horse. As Eisei said, it was just a coincidence; she had not been following them, and even if she had, he should be relieved she no longer was. After Ryusonji the lord was a hunted man, an outlaw. Any one of Aritomo's retainers might be on their trail, hoping to win the Minatogura lord's favor as well as great rewards. Maybe it was not a woman, at all, but a warrior in disguise. Maybe it was a mountain sorcerer or a witch.

But the foal knew her. He was certain of that.

How long was it since he had last been aware of her? He could not be sure. There was no way of knowing exactly what hour it was, with the sun hidden all day behind dense cloud. He was hungry enough for it to be almost evening, but he had been hungry since he woke, and the sparse dried meat and unripe yams had done little to fill his stomach. He walked for what seemed like a long time. The mare's cries grew fainter, and then he could no longer hear her at all, but the foal still trotted forward, stopping at every bend to check if Nagatomo was following.

The woman was sitting on a rock by the track, her head low, her face buried in her arms, her hands bound together in front of her. She did not move at their approach, but when the foal nuzzled her she put out her tied hands and pulled its head close to her. It allowed her to embrace it for a few moments, breathing out heavily. Then it nudged her more insistently. She raised her head slowly and looked at Nagatomo.

Her face was streaked with tears, her eyes and lips swollen with grief. He thought he must be an alarming sight, with the black face covering and his long sword and knife, but she showed no fear. In fact, she looked as if grief had consumed her and left no room for any other emotion.

He started to speak, but at that moment the foal squealed and leaped backward. The woman, as she fell, looked beyond Nagatomo, and he, forewarned by something in her eyes, had drawn his sword in an instant and turned to face his attackers.

One called, "Are you Kumayama no Kazumaru, known as Shikanoko, wanted for murder and rebellion?"

"Come and find out," Nagatomo said. He was assessing them quickly. They had emerged from the forest while he was distracted by the woman. How long had they been following them? Was she one of them, part of the trap? The foal whinnied and horses neighed in reply. The men wore crests of three pine trees on their jackets, and held swords, but they did not appear to have bows.

"It is he," the second man said. "He covers his face to hide the demon mask."

"There should be three horses," the first said, hesitating for one fatal moment, during which Nagatomo flew at him, flicking the man's sword from his hand with a twist of his own and with the returning stroke slicing him through the neck. The blood spurted from the opened artery, and the foal screamed like a human.

The second man, his eyes dark with shock, took a step back, gripping his sword. He was more prepared and, Nagatomo guessed, a better swordsman. He and Nagatomo circled each other, assessing stance, grip, weapon. Nagatomo's sword was longer and heavier. It gave him more reach, but his opponent's lighter blade gave its owner greater speed and flexibility. The other man was fitter, and probably better fed. Nagatomo wondered about him briefly, where he was from, what his name was, what fate had led them to encounter each other in the Darkwood, one evening in summer. Then he thought of nothing, as his enemy thrust at him and he began to fight for his life.

It had started to rain again and the ground was becoming slippery. For a long time they exchanged blows, parrying and ducking, grunting with exertion, now and then uttering cries of hatred. Nagatomo was slowly forcing the other back toward the stream, which was spilling over its banks and flooding onto the track. The water splashed around their ankles, hiding roots and holes, and one of these was his opponent's undoing. His foot slipped into it, he stumbled and dropped his guard.

Nagatomo rushed forward, the point of his sword entering the man's throat and coming out the other side, skewering him. The force of the blow threw the dying man backward into the water, his blood streaking the surface briefly, before becoming lost in the murky current.

Nagatomo put one foot on the man's chest, to pull out his weapon. Bubbles burst from the mouth and the wound. For a moment he thought the sword was stuck, but then it came free. His opponent's mouth under the water went slack and air no longer came from it, though blood did.

He staggered back to the bank, gasping for breath and trembling as the tension ebbed from his limbs. Elation seized him. He was not dead; his attackers were. He saw life and death, side by side, in their raw simplicity.

The foal came docilely to his side and sniffed at the man's legs. They looked foolish, half-covered by water. Nagatomo wanted to laugh; he wanted to embrace the foal. He gave it a thump on its hindquarters and turned to face the woman.

She was on her feet, her eyes fixed on him. He had hardly had time to look at her before. Now he studied her as he walked rapidly toward her, his eyes flicking over the undergrowth behind her in case there were any more men hidden there.

He stopped a few paces from her. She was tall, only a little shorter than he was, and large boned. Her face was tanned dark by the sun, her nose flat, her mouth wide. Her hair was covered by a sedge hat tied down by a scarf, but he guessed it would be as coarse as a horse's mane. It angered him irrationally that even a woman like this would never look on him with love or desire, and for that reason, or maybe because he suspected she had been in league with his attackers, he addressed her roughly.

"So you thought to entice me into an ambush? Your companions are dead. Who are you and why are you following us? Answer me truthfully or I'll send you to join them in the next world."

"They are no companions of mine," she said angrily. "They wear the crest of Matsutani—that means they serve Masachika. I was following the horses, and have been for weeks, ever since they were taken from Nishimi, when Masachika captured the Princess. I waited at Ryusonji. I saw you leave and watched you bury her. Then, when I realized Masachika's men were also on your trail, I stopped. I didn't want to lead them to you. I thought I might distract them while you vanished beyond their reach."

"And did you?" he said, unable to keep contempt from his voice.

"I think they were saving me for later," she said, without emotion. "That's why they tied me up." She held out her hands; he sheathed his sword, took out his knife, and cut the cords. The foal gave a low whinny, and, when her hands were free, she embraced it, as Nagatomo had wanted to earlier.

"Dear Tan," she said. "I never thought I would see you again."

"Tan?" he questioned. They had never given it a name; it was just called *the foal*.

"It's what my lady called him because when he was born he was as dark as coal. His coat is lightening now just as Saburo said it would." Her eyes filled with tears.

Nagatomo felt a perverse pang of jealousy. She was weeping for someone, in a way no one ever would for him. "So why follow us in the first place? You have not answered me."

"My name is Ibara. I have a favor to ask of you," she said, hesitant. "I am sorry, I know a woman like me should not speak so directly to a great warrior like yourself, but I am beyond caring about all that now."

One of the horses neighed from the grove.

"We should ride on," Nagatomo said. "Wait here while I get their horses. We will talk further as we ride."

The two horses were tethered beneath an oak tree. They laid back their ears at his approach and swung their haunches toward him, as though they would kick him, but the foal came barging through and its presence seemed to calm them. He untied them and led them back to the track, where he stripped the corpses of their clothes and footwear and gathered up the weapons, using one of the tethering cords to tie them into a bundle and strap them behind the saddle. Then he helped the woman mount one of the horses and, still holding its reins, leaped nimbly onto the back of the other.

"They are good horses," he exclaimed.

"Masachika is a rich man now," the woman replied. "The body of the Princess gained him many rewards."

"I imagine the favor you mean to ask is that we should kill him," Nagatomo said.

"Not exactly. I want you to teach me to fight with the sword, so I can kill him myself."

There was a clap of thunder and the rain began to fall more heavily.

It was nearly dusk when they caught up with Eisei, who had taken shelter beneath a rocky overhang, where the stream emerged from between steep cliffs. It offered some protection from the direct rain, but the walls and the boulders on the ground were dank with moisture. Farther back, a kind of low cave extended beneath the cliff, where the ground at least was dry.

"You can sleep here," Nagatomo told the woman, ignoring Eisei's disapproving look.

"Surely the lord . . ." she began.

"He will not sleep or seek shelter. We will take it in turn to keep watch."

"Where is he?" she said, gazing out at the rainy darkness.

Nagatomo looked at Eisei, who made a small movement with his shoulders and said, "Somewhere. Not far away, I think."

"What is wrong with him?" she said in a hesitant voice.

"He loved the Princess. She died," Eisei said curtly.

"He wants to die, too," the woman said, partly to herself. "I know that feeling." And then, even more quietly, so only Nagatomo heard her, "But we will see Masachika dead first."

❋

The horses were restless all night, upset by the two new stallions, who, excited by the presence of the mare, challenged Nyorin with loud calls. Bara hardly slept, and when she did, the dead talked to her in muffled voices and wrote messages she could not read. At dawn, she crawled from the cave and went toward the bushes. The man who had rescued her was asleep on his back. The other, the monk, was tending the smoky fire. Both had removed their face coverings and, after one shocked glance, she averted her gaze.

The monk did not look at her but, as she walked past, said, "See if you can find some dry wood."

"I will," she replied.

It had stopped raining and there were patches of blue sky overhead between the pink- and orange-tinged clouds. The foal came up to her eagerly and followed her through the undergrowth. Then it went ahead, while she squatted to relieve herself, turning back, when she stood, to whicker at her. The mare responded in the distance with an anxious neigh.

Bara walked after it. To her right, she could hear the endless babbling of the stream as it rushed over rocks and through pools. On her left, the forest rose in a steep slope, thick with trees she did not recognize, apart from maples. She had grown up in the port city of Akashi and then had worked in the house in Miyako, and the Nishimi palace, on the shore of the lake. Everything here alarmed her—the strange bird calls, the half-seen creatures that slithered away, the darkness between the trees that seemed to stretch away forever, the uncanny dappled circles where the sunlight shot through.

The ground was still sodden, but there were plenty of dead branches on tree trunks that she could reach easily, and she was breaking these off and making a bundle in her left arm when the foal, which had been walking ahead of her, stopped dead and snorted through its nose.

Pushing past it, she in turn halted suddenly. In the path stood the animal that she had noticed following the horses. She had thought it was a dog, but it did not look like any dog she had ever seen. Perhaps it was a wolf. Close up it did not seem quite real. Its eyes were as hard as gemstones and its movements awkward. The idea came to her that she was dreaming; she had fallen asleep, after all; she could almost feel the rocky floor of the cave beneath her. She struggled to wake. The wolf curled its painted lips, showing its carved teeth and its manlike tongue.

"Gen!" a low voice called, as if it were an angel or a demon, making a pronouncement. Shivers ran down her backbone. "Gen!"

The wolf seemed to sigh as it retreated. She went forward slowly, Tan's nose in her back, pushing her on.

She saw the head first and thought she had come upon a stag. The antlers, one broken, were lit up by the morning sun. Then she realized it was a man wearing a mask. She recognized the shape; it matched exactly the pattern of the burns on the other men's faces. It covered three quarters of his face, leaving his chin free. Through the sockets she could see his eyes, so black the iris and the pupil merged.

He had been sitting, his legs folded beneath him, but he stood as she approached. The antlers gave him added height and he seemed, to her, like some spirit of the forest, half man, half deer. He reminded her of the dancers at the summer festivals of her childhood. In Akashi they had danced the heron dance, wearing beaked and feathered headdress. In that garb, the men had become protective, chaste, quite unlike their usual truculent, predatory selves.

She felt no fear now, only pity, for somehow she recognized a grief as deep as her own.

He did not speak to her but addressed the foal.

"Who is this my lord has brought to me?"

She recognized the sword he wore at his hip—it was the sword the Princess had left in the shrine at Nishimi, as an offering to the Lake Goddess. He also bore a rattan bow and a quiver on his back, filled with arrows fletched with black feathers. She could see traces of cobwebs spun between them. It was a long time since they had been disturbed.

The foal nudged her, pushing her forward. She fell to her knees and said, "My name is Bara, but now I call myself Ibara. I was at Nishimi when the Princess came, with the horses and with that sword you wear."

A stillness came over him, like a deer after the first startle. She was afraid he was going to leap away and disappear into the forest, but then a long shudder ran through him and he sank to his knees in front of her.

"With Jato?" he touched its hilt briefly.

"If that is its name. The last time I saw it was before the altar in the shrine."

"Masachika must have taken it. It was made for me, but he had it at Matsutani. I took it back from him."

"You should have killed him then," Ibara said. "Swords return for a purpose."

He did not respond to this but said, "Tell me what happened at Nishimi."

She could see him more clearly now. How young he was! She had formed a picture of an older man, for that was what the word *lord* suggested to her. But he was not much more than a boy. How had he destroyed the Prince Abbot, in an act of such power the temple at Ryusonji had burned to the ground?

He loved the Princess. She died. His mouth had the same shape as little Take's, and his long fingers, too. Tears welled in her eyes.

"Akihime came to Nishimi, with Risu and Nyorin. Yukikuni no Takaakira employed me to look after Lady Hina. Hina knew the horses, she knew their names."

"Hina?" the lord said wonderingly. "Lord Kiyoyori's daughter?" And the foal came closer, nodding its head.

"I had no idea who Lady Hina was, other than that she was his ward and that he was secretive about her and didn't want anyone to know she was living with him. I guessed he'd saved her life. I would have done the same thing—anyone would. She was enchantingly pretty and so brave. She hid the Princess, and we pretended she had been rescued from the lake. After the baby was born Akihime worked in the kitchen. We thought no one would suspect her of being anything but a servant girl."

"She had a child?" His lips were ashen.

"A son. She wanted him to be called Takeyoshi. Lady Hina often played with him and she was carrying him when Masachika came over the mountains from the west." She halted abruptly. "This is the bit I don't understand. For he came with Saburo."

Tan gave a low whinny.

"Yes, Tan, Saburo, the man who saved your life at birth. He must have told Masachika that the Princess was at Nishimi, but I cannot believe he would betray her. And then Masachika killed him, stabbing him in the back."

"Masachika often works as a spy," the lord said.

"Your Saburo would not be the first to be deceived into trusting him."

He laid one hand against the foal's neck. "What happened to Hina?"

Ibara replied, "She jumped into the water with the baby in her arms."

Tears splashed on her arm and hand. The foal was weeping.

"What is this animal?" she cried, half-rising. "How does it understand every word and why is it shedding tears like a human?"

The lord said quietly, "The foal is a vessel for the spirit of Lord Kiyoyori, Hina's father."

"The one who died at the side of the Crown Prince? How can that be possible?"

He looked at her. The bone mask allowed no expression apart from the eyes, but they seemed to open onto a world she did not know existed. She could not hold his gaze.

"Is it like rebirth?" she said after a long silence.

"Not quite. Lord Kiyoyori's spirit refused to cross the river of death. A man who owed him an unthinkable debt took his place. I summoned the lord back. The mare was pregnant. His spirit took over the unborn foal."

It might have been the wild claim of a man driven mad by grief, yet, if she accepted it, so many things made sense—the foal's devotion to Hina, its ability to understand human speech, its tears.

"I don't believe Lady Hina is dead," she said, addressing the foal. "There was a boat. I think they saved her and the baby. Don't grieve for her yet . . ." And then, deeply uncomfortable, she added, "Lord."

Accepting it was true gave her new hope. "Why can't you summon the Princess back? Or Saburo? Summon him back into whatever shape you like. He died before we even held each other. I cannot stand it." She was twisting her hands together frantically.

"I know," he said, and, for a moment, Ibara felt their deep grief unite them. Then he said bitterly, "Don't think I haven't tried. Night after night, I attempt to walk again between the worlds and summon up the dead. But she is gone. Maybe she is in Paradise, maybe she is reborn, either way she is forever lost to me. Your Saburo must have died even earlier. He also will have crossed the last of the rivers that flow between this world and the next. I was given much power and taught many things, but I lay with her when I should not have done, and though together we destroyed the Prince Abbot, we did not escape punishment. She forfeited her life and I cannot remove the mask. I am condemned to live half animal, half human, belonging to neither world. I will go without food or sleep until I follow her into the realm of the dead. Maybe there I can find forgiveness."

"It is not forgiveness I seek," Ibara said in a low voice. "It is revenge."

The foal gave a sharp neigh of encouragement.

How strange, she thought, *I am just a girl from Akashi, a servant, but my desire for revenge is stronger than this boy's, who was born a lord, brought up as a warrior.*

41

"No one is to blame for the Princess's death but my-self," he said. "It is on myself that I am taking revenge."

"The baby looks like you. He is your son, isn't he? Don't you want to find him?"

"Better he died in the water," Shikanoko said, "than grow up in this world of sorrow."

3

MU

Three of the five boys who had been born from cocoons, Mu, Ima, and Ku, had been left at the mountain hut all winter. Once a messenger had come from Shikanoko at Kumayama to check that they were still alive, but after that they heard nothing of him or their other brothers, Kiku and Kuro. At first they did not worry, living day to day without much thought, like animals, but when spring came Mu began to be plagued by restlessness and a sort of anxiety. He took to roaming through the Darkwood and it was there that he saw a foxes' wedding, though at the time he did not know what it was. It was the third month, when showers chased sunshine. For several days he had been away from the hut, sleeping under the stars or in caves when it was too wet, feeling almost like a fox himself. One morning he was plucking young fern shoots, cramming the tender stems into his mouth, in one of the hidden clearings on the lower slopes of Kuroyama, when he heard curious noises, the soft padding of many feet and flute music, so high he could not tell if it was really music or the wind in the pine trees, and drums that might have been rain falling. He quickly climbed an oak tree and hid in the foliage as a procession came into the clearing.

At first, he thought they were people, dressed in colorful clothes, walking upright, playing flutes and drums, but then he saw their pointed ears, their black-tipped snouts, their precise, delicate paws. A male and a female were carried on the shoulders of the largest foxes, who were the size of wolves. Like the music, they hovered between reality and imagination, filling him with an intense longing. He did not think they were aware of him, but, as they passed beneath the oak tree, one young female looked up and smiled in his direction, a smile that seemed to be an invitation into worlds he had not known existed.

The sun shone brilliantly on the short winter grass, only recently liberated from snow, starred with flowers, yellow aconites and celandines, white anemones. The bride and groom were lowered to the ground and stood facing each other. They joined hands—*paws*, Mu thought—as the flutes played even more sweetly and the drums more loudly. Then the sky darkened, sudden rain joined in the drumming, and, when Mu could see again, they had all disappeared, as if the shower had dissolved them.

When he came home his brothers Kiku and Kuro had returned and were crouched by the fire, silent and miserable. He felt a moment of relief, as if his anxiety had been for them, but why had they come alone and why did they look like that? The youngest brother, Ku, was sitting near them, watching them with a troubled expression on his face, a bunch of puppies, as usual, crawling over him and tumbling around him. The fourth boy, Ima, was tending a pot in which a stew of spring shoots was simmering along with some sort of meat.

Ima scooped broth into wooden bowls and offered them to Kiku and Kuro. Kuro took one and drank without a word, but Kiku refused with a gesture that made Mu's heart sink.

"What's happened?" he said.

"Shikanoko . . ." Kuro began.

"Don't you dare speak!" Kiku shouted. "It was all your fault!" He hit Kuro over the shoulders so violently the soup flew from the bowl, scalding Kuro's face and hands. Kuro swore, grabbed a smoldering stick from the fire, and thrust it toward Kiku's face.

"Stop it, stop it!" Mu cried. "What happened to Shikanoko? He's not dead?"

"He might as well be," Kiku said angrily. "He has sent us away. He never wants to see us again. It was all Kuro's stupid fault. I told him to leave all his creatures behind. But he had to bring the deadliest one."

"The snake? The snake bit someone?" Mu said.

"Only a woman." Kuro tried to defend himself.

"Only a woman?" Kiku repeated. "The woman we were meant to rescue, the Autumn Princess, the woman Shika loved."

"I don't understand that," Kuro muttered. "I don't know what *love* means."

"I'm not sure I do either," Kiku admitted.

Mu thought of the fox girl and how her look had transfixed him. *Do I love her?* he wondered.

"Shika felt something for her," Kiku tried to explain. "An emotion so strong her death destroyed him. He has turned us away, our older brother, our father, the only one who cared for us, who brought us up." He said all this in a bewildered voice as though, for the first time in his life, he himself was feeling some strong emotion. He brushed his hand against his eyes. "What is this? Is it the smoke making my eyes water?"

Tears were staining his cheeks. Mu could not remember ever seeing him cry, not even when the rest of them had wept after Shisoku died. "Where has Shika gone?" he said.

Kiku sniffed. "He rode away into the Darkwood, with Gen, three horses, and two men with burnt faces. He performed an act of great magic and defeated the priest. He raised a dragon child from the lake. You should have seen it, Mu, it was magnificent. Balls of lightning everywhere, a roaring like you've never heard. The priest dissolved in fire."

"Tell Mu about the price Shika paid," Kuro said. "Tell him about the mask."

"The stag mask he uses," Kiku said. "It stuck to his face. It cannot be taken off. Now he is half man and half deer."

"Is that so bad?" Mu asked, wishing he could be half fox.

"It would not matter if he had stayed with us." Kiku gestured toward the fake animals that the old mountain sorcerer Shisoku had created from skins and skeletons. "He would have fitted in perfectly here. Or he could still have been a warlord like he intended. He would have been all the more terrifying. He did not need to send us away. He could have achieved anything he wanted with our help. Look what we have done for him so far! He would never have got the better of that monk, Gessho, or taken his old home back from his uncle."

"It was my bee that killed the uncle," Kuro added proudly.

"And then getting into Ryusonji," Kiku continued. "It's a shame about the Princess—my eyes are doing that strange thing again. Why is your fire so smoky, Ima?—but the Prince Abbot was destroyed. Shika could have done none of those things without us."

At that moment one of the fake wolves gave a long, muffled howl and fell over with a thump. Ku pushed away the pile of dogs that surrounded him and ran to it. The puppies yelped and snarled at it in playful attacks, but it did not move. The other boys stared at it.

"It's dead," Ku said.

"It was never really alive." Kuro moved toward it and knelt beside it, pushing the puppies away. He looked up at Kiku. "Whatever power was holding it together has left it."

Kiku looked wildly around at the other fake animals, making no effort now to control his tears. Mu followed his gaze. He realized what he had not noticed before: Shisoku's creations were winding down, fading in some way. Regret stabbed him. He also felt his eyes water. Why hadn't he looked after them better?

A crow plummeted from the branch it had been perched on and lay broken and silent on the ground, its borrowed feathers scattered by the breeze.

"No!" Kiku sobbed.

"You never liked them much, anyway," Mu said, surprised at his apparent sorrow.

"I hate them," Kiku replied, controlling himself with an effort. "But they are breaking down before I've had a chance to learn how they work, how to make them. How did Shisoku get them to move, to live to the extent they did? How did he and Shika make the mask? What would he have done with the monk's skull that we buried? And the horse's? I need to learn all these things, and now there is no one to teach me."

"What's going to happen to us?" Ima said, suddenly anxious.

Kuro said, "The old man Sesshin . . ."

Mu started at the name. "He is one of our fathers. The only one still alive, apart from Shika."

"Well, he told Shika to kill us. He called us imps. My snake was meant to bite him!"

"He must know some sorcery," Kiku said.

"He gave all his power away to Shika," Kuro said. "I heard the torturers tell the Abbot Prince."

"Prince Abbot," Kiku corrected him.

"Whatever, he is gone." Kuro stood up. "But wasn't

the dragon superb? If only I could learn to summon one up like that."

"Well, you won't now," Kiku retorted. "Because Shika is never going to want to see you again."

They looked wildly at one another. They were all crying now, even Kuro.

What will become of us? Mu thought. *There is no one in the world who cares about us.*

❄

Over the next few weeks the boys sulked and squabbled as more of Shisoku's animals ran out of living force and fell to the ground. Mu wanted to burn them; they did not exactly decay like real animals, but they gave out a strange smell; insects began to dwell in the hides and maggots hatched. The corpses heaved with a new movement that nauseated him. But Kiku would not allow it. He studied each one's unique makeup, committing to memory how they were put together, out of which materials.

He went through the hut, looking at, smelling, tasting the contents of all the flasks of potions and jars of incense and ointments that Shisoku had concocted or collected. The sorcerer had kept records in an arcane script, which none of them could read, but Kiku searched out every object of power, every amulet and statue and figurine. He knew their weight and what they were made from, but he did not know how to use them for his own ends. That did not stop him trying everything out, experimenting fearlessly.

Sometimes he raved uncontrollably about visions and deep insights, sometimes he seemed to work magic by accident. Once he threw up so violently and for so long the others thought he was dying.

He gathered the remains of the werehawk, from where they still lay on the roof, and made a necklace from the beak and talons. He dug up the horse's skull. Worms and insects had done their work and the flesh was stripped from the bone. The last remnants fell away when Kiku boiled the skull in an iron pot on the fire.

"You can't make a horse," Mu said. "Even Shisoku never made anything so large."

"I want to make a mask like Shika's," Kiku replied.

Mu had never seen the mask, only knew the seven-layered brocade bag in which it used to be kept, but Kiku had watched Shika wear it and had held it in his hands.

"I carried it," he said, with a note of pride in his voice. "He said he wanted to leave it behind, but I knew he didn't really, so I took it to him."

He described it to Mu: the stag's skull, the antlers, one broken, the half-human, half-animal face with its carved features, smoothly lacquered, and its cinnabar-reddened lips. But he did not know the ritual in which it had been created, months before the boys were born, the blending of the red and white essences of male and female.

When the horse head was reduced to gleaming bone, Kiku tried to shape it, but his chisel often slipped and the resulting skull pan was lopsided and jagged. He made a face mask from wood, carving out eye sockets and a mouth hole, and he and Kuro lacquered it without really knowing the method. The lacquer bubbled and cracked, as if it were diseased, and the result was monstrous, both laughable and sinister. When Kiku put it on, the dogs howled and ran to Ku, and two more fake animals lay down and did not get up again.

"It's useless," Kiku said, taking the mask off and throwing it to the ground. "It's ugly and it has no power."

"It's only your first attempt," Mu said. "Imagine how many times Shisoku had to experiment and practice before he got it right. And he was still making mistakes up to the time he died."

"But he mostly knew what he was doing. He must have had so much knowledge," Kiku said. "Why do I have no one to teach me? Don't you ever feel it? That there is a huge part of our lives missing? Why is there no one like us? Where did they all go?" He sighed, and glanced around the clearing, his eyes falling on the dogs, cowering around his youngest brother. "Maybe the skull has to come from something I kill myself."

"No!" Ku said defiantly.

"A dog is too easy," Mu added. "It is not enough of a challenge for you." He picked up the horse mask and set it on a pole near the hut. "It'll make a good guard."

The mask was not what Kiku had intended, yet it was not a complete failure, and some strange force had attached itself to it. At night they heard hoofbeats and whinnying, and several times, the post seemed to have

moved by morning. Ima was fascinated by it. He patted
the post and clicked his tongue at it when he went past,
and brought offerings of fresh grass and water.

Weeks went by. Shikanoko did not return. Kiku continued his experiments. Kuro set about replacing his col-
lection of poisonous creatures, and managed to capture
another sparrow bee.

One morning Mu had gone with Ima to the stream
to gather grass and check the fish traps. The boys were
always hungry, and although they preferred meat to
fish, fish were easier to get and more plentiful. The
stream did not flood that spring and, in the deep pools,
sweetfish hid in the shadows, while crabs could be
found under every rock. Sometimes the traps would
catch an eel, which was as rich and tasty as meat. They
were both knee-deep in the water when they heard
someone approaching. Neither of them had Kiku's acute
hearing, but the sounds were unmistakable: a snapped
twig, a dislodged stone, and then a quickly muffled gasp
as a foot slipped. The two boys were out of the water
and into the undergrowth in one movement, as quick as
lizards.

A boy and a girl came warily down to the stream.
The boy looked familiar, and Mu realized it was the
messenger who had been sent by Shikanoko in the winter,
the boy called Chika. He was still not very clear about
human ages—his own growth, like all his brothers',
had been so rapid he had nothing to go by—but he knew
Chika was a boy, definitely not yet a man. The girl seemed
younger, but maybe not by much. They were both thin,

legs scratched and bleeding in several places, barefoot, burned brown by the sun. Yet the boy carried a sword, and the girl a knife, and, Mu thought, they both looked as if they knew how to use them.

The boy knew his way, leading the girl across the stream, helping her jump from boulder to boulder. When they reached the bank, they walked downstream toward the hut. Mu picked up the fish they had already caught, still flapping on the grass stem threaded through their gills, and gestured to Ima to bring the bucket of crabs. They followed the pair, silent and unseen.

The boy halted near the horse skull, hand on sword, and called, "Is anyone there? I am Chikamaru, son of Kongyo, from Kuromori. I am looking for the man known as Shikanoko."

Kiku emerged from the hut, blinking in the sunlight. "We know who you are, Chika. Shikanoko is not here."

Slowly the other boys appeared and surrounded the pair. The girl held her knife out threateningly, but Kiku brushed it aside and stepped close to her, touching her face and her hair, in a gentle way that both astonished and alarmed Mu.

"Kongyo?" Kiku said finally. "He was the man who came with the horse." His eyes flickered to the horse mask on the pole.

Chika said, "That's Ban? My father said he died. He was our last horse. But what have you done to his skull?"

Kiku made a dismissive gesture. "It doesn't matter."

The girl began to cry silently, as if the sight of the

horse, once no doubt magnificent and prized, now a hideous replica, had unleashed all her grief.

"I've done that," Kiku told her. "Water has come from my eyes. It will dry up, don't worry."

His face had taken on an intense fixed expression, like a male animal about to mate or kill.

"Cook the fish," Mu said to Ima, to break the uncomfortable silence, and then addressed the boy, Chika. "Sit down, we'll eat something. Are you hungry?"

They both nodded. The girl slumped down, still weeping. Chika said, "Our mother told us to flee. After our father died she was afraid his murderers might seek to kill us, too. I don't know what will happen to her. My sister is still in shock, I think. She hardly speaks and the slightest thing sets off her tears."

"Our mother is dead," Kiku said, sitting down next to the girl. "She died just after we were born."

"Lady Tora?" Chika said.

The boys stared at him. "You knew our mother?" Mu said.

"She came to Matsutani with Akuzenji, the King of the Mountain. Shikanoko was with them, too."

Mu remembered the name, Akuzenji. Shika had told them he was one of their five fathers.

"What does that mean, King of the Mountain?" said Kiku.

"That's what he called himself. He wasn't really a king, he was a bandit. Merchants paid him so they could travel safely along the northern highway. If they didn't pay, he robbed them and usually killed them. He set an ambush for Lord Kiyoyori, whom my father served, but he was captured and the lord beheaded him and all his men, except Shikanoko. Then Lord Kiyoyori fell madly in love with Lady Tora and made her his mistress, even though she was said to be a sorceress."

"One of our fathers took the head of another of them," Kiku murmured. "That would be a skull worth having."

"The bodies were burned and the heads displayed at the borders of the estate," Chika said. "You should have seen it—thirty men separated from their heads in as many minutes. It was brutal. I've been in sieges and battles, but nothing was as horrifying as that day."

"You say you have been in battles," Mu said, "but you are not yet a grown man."

"I still know how to fight with this." Chika tapped the sword that lay beside him on the grass. "I have just escaped from the battle in which my father died."

"Why have you come here?" Ima said from the fire. The sweet smell of grilling fish rose in the air.

"I could think of nowhere else to go. Our father is dead, along with all Lord Kiyoyori's men and their families. We held out for months in the fortress at Kuromori, but after Shikanoko left for the capital, and never came back, Lord Masachika attacked for the second time, took the fortress, and put all the defenders to death. Then he did the same at Kumayama. He holds a huge domain now for the Miboshi. No one is left to oppose him in all the east."

"It sounds very complicated," Kiku said. "You'll have

to explain it to us. We need to understand all these things, if we are to live in the world."

"No one understood why Shikanoko disappeared," Chika said. "They felt betrayed and abandoned. At first we thought he must have died, but then we heard that he destroyed the Prince Abbot at Ryusonji. He could have dominated the capital himself, but he rode away, no one knows where."

"Someone died," Kiku said, glancing at Kuro, who sat a little way off, letting a snake slither up his arms and around his neck. "A girl Shika liked."

"Loved," Mu said.

Kiku frowned. "Loved," he repeated, and bent forward to look in the girl's face. She squirmed away and said to her brother, "I don't want to stay here."

"You spoke," he said in delight. "You see, we will be safe here. We can stay, can't we?"

"Of course," Kiku said. "You are welcome, you and your sister. What did you call her?"

"Kaze."

"And your name, Chika—that's like the other lord you mentioned."

"Masachika. I wish it were not. I hate him more than any man alive. It's one of the clan names—Chika, Masa, Kiyo, Yori. Many of us are called some variation of it. Masachika is Lord Kiyoyori's younger brother."

So he is some relation to us, Mu thought. *If Kiyoyori is one of our fathers, this Masachika is our uncle. Kaze is Chika's sister. He will be uncle to her children. And if I have children my brothers will be their uncles.* He thought of the foxes and the girl he had seen, thought of having children with her. The blood rushed to his face and he trembled. In the following weeks he often went back to the clearing, looking for her, but he did not find her.

❋

During that time Kiku and Chika had many conversations about the realm and governance of the Eight Islands: the emperor, the nobility, the great families who held roles of state, the warlords and their warriors, the rich merchants who had their own sort of power. Kiku's frustration increased daily, until finally he announced his intention to go out into the strange and enticing world Chika described. "You can't be a sorcerer without someone to teach you," he said. "We can't live in this stinking place forever. We must find some way of having power in the world."

"Maybe we should be bandits," Kuro said. "I would like to be called King of the Mountain."

"King of the Insects, that's what you are," Ku jeered.

"And you are King of the Dogs," Kuro countered.

"Bandits are like crows," Kiku said. "They swoop down and steal, they scavenge. But if you are rich you don't have to scavenge."

"Others steal from you, then," Mu said.

"Then you could be a bandit, in secret, as well as a merchant," Kiku suggested. "Yes, that's what I would like to be."

"Being a warrior sounds very fine," said Ima, who

had been entranced by Chika's tales of heroism and sacrifice.

"You can't be a warrior," Chika told him. "You have to be born into a clan."

"Lord Kiyoyori was our father," Ima reminded him. "And so was Shika."

"Well, if Shikanoko had stayed around he might have brought you up as warriors. But he's disappeared and Lord Kiyoyori is dead, and no one's going to believe you're sons of either of them."

"Why not?" Ku asked.

"You don't look like it," Chika replied.

"What do we look like?" said Kiku.

"Not like anyone else, really," the warrior's son said.

The brothers exchanged glances, seeing one another's coppery skin, their sharp bony faces, their unkempt black hair.

"I have no intention of being a warrior," Kiku declared. "They all end up being killed or killing themselves. I am going to be a merchant by day, and a bandit by night. And maybe a spy or an assassin, but only for the highest reward."

Chika laughed. "To be a merchant you have to have something to sell, and ways of either making it or buying it."

Kiku laughed, too, but more loudly. "I have something that I think will get me started. Come into the hut."

They crowded into the hut after him and watched as he pulled a pile of old rags away from the wall. Beneath it lay a large flat stone.

"I'd never been able to move it," Kiku said. "Then, one day, it shifted. Something I did must have unlocked it. Help me lift it—Kuro, you're the strongest."

Together, they raised the stone and slid it aside. A wooden chest had been buried under it. Kiku removed the lid and plunged both hands in, pulling out pearls, golden statues, silver prayer beads, copper coins, jade carvings—all small, light things that could be easily carried. "They must be valuable," he said.

"Where did it come from?" Kuro asked.

"Maybe Akuzenji got the sorcerer to hide it for him?" Mu suggested.

"That's what I think," Kiku said. "Our fathers provided for us, before they knew of our existence. It's touching, isn't it, Chika?"

Chika said nothing, just stared at the treasure.

"What should I deal in, Chika? You know what men buy and sell. What are the things people cannot do without?"

"Wine, I suppose, and the things you make from soybeans: paste, curds, sauce."

"I imagine I'll find out what all that stuff is," Kiku said. "Chika and I will go to . . . what's the best place?"

"Maybe Kitakami," Chika said. "I've never been there, but it has the reputation of being a city where anyone can make a fortune. It trades with countries on the mainland. It is said to be rough and wild."

"Then we will go to Kitakami."

"I don't mind coming with you," Chika said. "But what about Kaze?"

"Kaze can stay here. I'll come back for her once I've started making my fortune."

"I'm coming with you, too," Kuro announced.

Kiku stared at him for a moment, and then nodded. "Yes, I'm sure I'll need you."

Kuro grinned. "Me and my creatures."

※

After the three left, Mu, Ima, and Ku went back to the peaceful life they had been leading before their brothers returned. Yet it was not quite the same, for now they had a girl living with them. She followed Ku and the dogs around and joined Ima in bringing offerings to the skull of her father's horse. She ate what they ate and slept alongside them, outside on fine nights, inside the hut when it rained. It did not rain often—even though the plum rains should have set in—and the days and nights were very hot.

Shikanoko had taught all the boys to use the bow. One day, Kaze took up Mu's bow, went off into the forest, and returned with a hare and two squirrels. They could all move silently, and could take on invisibility, but she was a better shot than any of them. She still did not speak much, but now and then, at the end of the day when they sat around the fire watching the flames grow brighter as night fell, she would sing—lullabies that made the dogs sigh in their sleep, ballads of love and courage that filled the boys with yearning.

They were fascinated and intimidated by her. She ordered them around, as if it were her right to be served.

Ku and Ima adored her. Her presence, Mu thought, made them all more gentle, more complex—perhaps more like real people. He remembered Shika's wolf companion, Gen, who had been as artificial as the ones whose remains now littered the clearing, but who had grown more and more real because of its attachment to its master.

He began to pay more attention to the fake animals, tried to revive their strange spark of life.

Even objects need attention, he thought. *Even the lifeless need love.*

Some nights, he saw green eyes shine in the darkness under the trees and he imagined the foxes had come to listen to the singing. He heard vixens scream at midnight. One day, when he went to the stream to get water, a fox was drinking from one of the pools. It ran into the undergrowth at his approach. He called, without knowing why, "Come back! I won't hurt you!" and a few moments later the leaves rustled and the fox girl stepped out.

They stood and gazed at each other, the stream flowing sluggishly between them. She seemed less like a fox than before and more like a human. Her ears were only slightly pointed and her feet were small and delicate, but they were definitely feet, not paws. Beneath her robe, which was dyed red and tied with a yellow sash, was a hint of a tail, but, at second glance, it was not a tail at all but just the way the robe fell.

"I saw you," he said.

"I know. You were in the oak tree."

"What was it?"

"A wedding," she said gravely. "I'll show you if you like."

He held out his hand. "Come across."

"No, you come to me," she commanded.

He leaped the stream in a bound and found himself so close to her he could smell her faint animal scent. She smiled at him and, reaching up—she was much smaller than he was—kissed him on the mouth.

The effect on him was so surprising he broke away from her, crying out, which made her laugh. Taking his hand, she led him into the bushes and pulled him down, so they were lying side by side. The sunlight dappled the moss with tiny circles. In the distance a warbler was calling. She loosened her robe and guided his hands to her body, then reached under his clothes to caress him.

❋

She lived in the hut with him as his wife. She combed and braided Kaze's hair—the girl responded as if the fox woman were her mother, climbing on her knee when they sat by the fire, though Kaze was really too big to be cuddled. The dogs growled at her at first, but she rubbed their ears, picked off their fleas, and won them over. She was always merry; everything made her laugh. She liked to dance in the twilight, while Kaze sang. And every night she lay down with Mu and made him happy in a way he had never dreamed of.

Once he said to her, "Why did you choose me?"

"Your mother was one of the Old People."

"I don't know what that means," he said.

"They were here before the horsemen came. They are more like us, both animal and human. Shisoku was one, too. The Old People know many things about other realms that the horse people have never learned."

Mu thought about the mask and the skulls. "Can you teach me those things?"

"I am teaching you already," she said, laughing. "Didn't you notice?"

4

SHIKANOKO

Throughout the summer the Burnt Twins and Shika-noko kept traveling north, following the tracks of deer and foxes through the tangled forest. Not knowing where else to go, Ibara went with them. They saw no one nor was there any sign that they were being followed.

That first autumn the rain ceased and though the following winter there were heavy snowfalls, the seasonal summer rains failed. They had found shelter in an abandoned building where a solitary hermit had once lived. It stood near a spring from which water flowed constantly, and the former occupant had made a garden, which still existed wild and overgrown. Yams and taro had self-seeded, as well as pumpkins, and there were fruit trees, an apricot and a loquat. They found his bones in the garden, in a tangle of grass and kudzu vine, scattered by scavenging birds and animals. Eisei gathered them up and buried them.

Animals came to drink at the spring, foxes, wolves, and deer. The deer lingered to graze on the sweet grass in the clearing, which, thanks to the spring, flourished all through the hot summers while the rest of the land dried up. Nagatomo trapped hares and rabbits and shot birds—pigeons mostly and the occasional pheasant—but the lord would not allow them to hunt deer. Consequently the deer became more and more tame, allowing him to mingle with them and feeding from his hand.

"That is why he is called Shikanoko," Nagatomo said. "The deer's child."

Ibara had not known his name, though she had heard it once, a long time ago, it seemed, from the mouth of the man with the Matsutani crest whom Nagatomo had killed. In the long months when there was little to do, Nagatomo taught her with that dead man's weapons and now she carried his sword at her hip; she wore his clothes and tied her hair back. She had fallen a little in love with Nagatomo, almost overcome with desire when he held her hips or shoulders to correct her stance, but he never responded. She knew he and the monk were lovers, twinned in some way by their shared suffering. In time she recovered her equilibrium, but she did not lose her desire for revenge. Every day she thought of Masachika and how she was going to kill him.

Shikanoko spent hours in meditation, but he began to eat. Ibara could feel how, little by little, grief gave up its grip on her heart, and she thought she could sense the same in him. When the deer came in the evening he moved among them as if he were following the steps of an ancient dance. When she had first seen him she had recalled the heron dancers. Now he danced with the deer—they all did—and in the dance created the ties that bind Heaven and Earth, humans and animals, the living and the dead.

The foal grew to its full size and its dark coat turned to silver. It looked like its father but had a black mane and tail. Nagatomo introduced it to the saddle and bridle, but it did not need breaking in. It accepted the saddle but did not like to be bridled. However, no one felt comfortable riding it. There were enough horses for the three men, and Ibara took Risu. Tan followed close by her side and she talked to him about Hina, feeling sorry for the man trapped in a horse's body, wondering what good it had done him to be summoned back.

The mare lay down one cold winter night and did not get up again. The death rekindled Shika's grief and he wept bitterly. The two stallions mourned like humans.

Something about Ibara's presence goaded Shika-noko. She was like the thorn she had named herself. She pricked and scratched away at the armor he was building around himself. Perhaps it was that she often talked of Hina to the horse Tan, and then she would mention Tan's twin, his own son, Takeyoshi. So he heard of the baby's birth, and Hina's beauty, her great intelligence, her kindness, and it filled him with a longing to see them both.

It was not magic or sorcery, nor did she do it deliberately, but little by little he awakened and began to emerge from grief. He took out Jato and cleaned and polished it, rebound his bow, Kodama, and carved new arrows, fletching them with white winter plumage.

They were in the northernmost part of the Darkwood, right up near the Snow Country. The snow was heavier than Shika had ever seen. After blizzards they had to dig their way out of the hut. The clearing, the grave, every branch and twig, every boulder and rock was blanketed in white.

For weeks they were confined inside together. On the worst nights they brought the horses inside, too, otherwise they would have been buried under the snow. Shika's intention had been, when winter came, to continue his meditation and fasting in the open, which was really a slow way of killing himself, fading back into the forest, ceasing to live in a world so full of pain. But perversely his body showed signs of wanting to live. It became hungry and demanded food; suddenly it slept again, in the deep, healing sleep of boyhood. His mind awoke, too. His hours of solitary meditation had revealed to him, among other things, how little he knew. He understood nothing about how the world worked, what Aritomo's motives were, why the Miboshi and the Kakizuki fought each other, what it meant to be a warrior, what the nature of revenge, such as Ibara desired, was. He recalled his own upbringing, his father's death, up here in the north; the loss of the bow, Ameyumi; his uncle's brutality. And now he had a son, Takeyoshi, whom he was condemning to the same orphan state.

He saw how impetuous and thoughtless his actions had been, all his life, how he had been used and manipulated by others, for both good and bad, in his need for approval and affection, in his quest to redress his own pain.

On days when the snow fell heavily, there was nothing to do but talk. Eisei had received the usual education of a monk, could read and write, and knew sutras and other holy writings by heart. He had also absorbed, over the years, the songs and ballads that were sung in the outer courtyards at Ryusonji, and he often recited these: long, intricate tales of heroes, warriors, powerful priests, warring clans, child emperors. Nagatomo and Shika had shared the rudimentary education of provincial warriors. They could read and write, and knew the history of their clan and the legends of Kumayama, but they had never learned how to conduct a careful argument or correct a false idea. Ibara could read a little, write in women's script, and calculate. She knew a great deal about her hometown, Akashi, and the way the free port and its merchants operated. Since she did not defer to any of them, dressed like a man, and usually spoke like one, they forgot she was a woman. Three of them were born in the same year. Nagatomo was a year older.

One evening, Ibara said, "Takaakira, the man who employed me to look after Lady Hina, was called the Lord of the Snow Country. I suppose his estates were not far from here?"

"We are alongside them," Nagatomo replied. "They

begin on the eastern edge of the Darkwood and extend far to the north."

Shika recalled the day Eisei had told him of Takaa-kira's death. He had not known then that it was on Hina's account. Now he felt a new interest in the man who, in disobeying Aritomo, had saved Hina's life and paid for it with his own.

"What sort of a man was he?" he asked Ibara.

"In truth, I hardly spoke to him, and then only about Hina. He knew a great deal about all sorts of things; he wrote poetry. There were two women whom he ar-ranged to instruct Hina in history, music, and so on. He talked more to them, about her progress and her timetables. I had no idea a child could absorb so much. It used to worry me sometimes. I had to make sure she went outside from time to time, even though he didn't really approve. He wanted her to keep her pale complexion."

"He had a reputation for courage," Nagatomo said.

"I heard him claim once he was an adept," Eisei added. "There must be some strange esoteric practices in the Snow Country. He believed Yoshimori was the true emperor and he was going to tell Aritomo that on the day he died, and plead for your life and the Princess's. I suppose he never got the chance."

Ibara had a remote expression on her face as if she was dwelling on the past. "He adored her," she said finally. "I've never seen a man so obsessed."

Shika was surprised at the strong emotion that welled up in him, part jealousy, part affront, but also, mingled in, gratitude and relief. Before he met Ibara, he had assumed Hina had died in the massacre of the Kakizuki women and children. Now Ibara was convinced she had not drowned. But where had she gone? What had happened to her?

"Yet she was only a child," he said. "And how old was he?"

"Well over thirty, I would imagine," Ibara replied. "She was about eleven years old. He intended to make her his wife—but he had not touched her," she added, maybe noticing Shika's face.

The shutters rattled as the wind howled against them. The snow fell with the lightest of sounds, like insects swarming.

✳

On sunny days, when the snow did not fall, they rode out through the forest—no longer the dark wood but gleaming white. The horses plunged through the deep snow, snorting with excitement. Gen was light enough to run over the frozen surface. They took their bows and hunted hares and squirrels. Sometimes they saw wolf tracks. Every now and then, Shika caught sight of his antlered shadow, blue-black on the snowy ground. Each time he felt the shock anew.

Will I ever be rid of it?

As spring approached, the snow fell with rain mixed in. The icicles that clung to the roof began to drip in the sun. The stream melted and the water roared with its new fierce flow. The deer dropped their antlers.

Nagatomo and Ibara collected them, polishing them. Fawns were born, and bounded after their mothers on long, delicate legs.

The short summer brought biting flies and heavy humid air. Violent thunderstorms crackled round the mountain peaks. In the autumn, drums sounded from far away, giving a rhythm to their own dances. Another winter passed: the same deep drifts of snow, the same long conversations in the smoky hut. They saw no one else and began to forget they were fugitives. No one ventured so deep into the forest, or so they thought, until one day in early spring when Nagatomo returned from collecting water, saying, "Am I going mad and hearing things, or is someone beating a drum in the distance?"

Once he mentioned it, they all heard it, a dull, monotonous pounding on a solitary drum. It stopped for a while, then started up again. It was the wrong time of year for the drum festivals and, in truth, the playing did not sound skillful.

"Someone practicing?" Ibara suggested.

After the drumming had persisted for a full day and a half, Shika said, "I'm going to see what it is."

The Burnt Twins exchanged a swift look, and said together, "We should go."

"You still act as if it matters whether I live or die," Shika said, with amusement.

"It matters to us," Nagatomo said.

Shika was touched, though he did not show it. "Well, you can come with me. Ibara, do you mind keeping guard here?"

The drumbeat was halting and uncertain, yet there was something compelling about it. The mask responded to it in some way. He felt the rhythm pass through his skull and reverberate within the antlers.

The snowmelt filled the streams and the trees were just beginning to put on their first green sheen. Frogs rejoiced and birds sang, skirmished, mated in their urge to raise young ones before the short summer ended. The horses trotted eagerly, nipping at one another and bucking occasionally for the sheer joy of being alive.

On the edge of the forest, where the huge trees gave way to bamboo groves and then to coppice, the stream widened into a marshy lake. Sedge and susuki reeds grew around it; a snipe took off at their approach with a sudden cry of alarm.

A shaggy northern pony, dun colored with a brown mane and tail, threw up its head from where it had been grazing and whinnied loudly. The drumbeat stopped abruptly. A young boy, about ten years old, got to his feet, took one look at the antlered man on the white horse, and ran away, shouting to the pony to come to him. But he was slowed by the drum and Nagatomo easily caught up with him before he could reach his mount.

He tried to lean over and scoop up boy and drum together, but his horse was spooked by the drum's hollow sound against its neck, and shied, throwing its rider. Nagatomo fell to the ground, still holding the boy, the silk covering slipping from his face.

When he stood, the boy looked up at his ruined features but did not say a word. Nagatomo's horse ran back to the others. Eisei seized its reins. The boy's eyes followed it, he saw Eisei's black-covered face, and then he saw Shika. He tried to wriggle out of Nagatomo's grasp, not to escape but to throw himself facedown on the ground.

"Kamisama, kamisama," he wailed. "Please help me!"

Shika dismounted and told him to sit up. It saddened him to see the fear and shock in the boy's face.

"I am no god," he said, thinking, *But I will never be human again.*

"Then take off the mask," the boy challenged.

"That I cannot do."

"Then you must be gods or spirits, all of you. I was trying to summon the deer god. I didn't really think I could, but I was so desperate I didn't know what else to do. And you came."

"Is that why you were beating the drum?" Eisei said.

The boy replied, "People have said they've seen a figure, part deer, part man, in the forest. I thought I would try to call him out. I borrowed the drum from the shrine, but it's not as easy to make it speak as I thought it would be."

"You were certainly persistent," Nagatomo remarked. "In what way do you need help?"

"My father died two years ago in Miyako, and now his cousins want to divide his estate among them. They say he was ordered to take his own life because he was a traitor and therefore his lands must be forfeited and I should not inherit them. When my mother opposes them, they say she and I deserve death, too, and we will be killed if we do not submit. But my mother thinks we will be killed even if we do. There is no one to help us. We cannot appeal to Lord Aritomo—my mother suspects he might even be supporting these false claims."

"What was your father's name?" Shika said, though he had already guessed the answer.

"Yukikuni no Takaakira, Lord of the Snow Country. My name is Takauji. I am his only son." He had recovered some of his composure and now studied them, with their ragged clothes and their wild hair and beards, almost insolently. "You are so few. And you look like bandits. Is this how the deer god answers my prayers?"

Shika liked his defiant attitude and found himself inclined to help Takaakira's son. He put his hand on Jato and felt the sword quiver in response, as if it sensed his desire to fight and shared it.

"There is one more of us," he said. "We are not bandits, but you are right, we are few. How many cousins are there, and what forces do they command?"

"There are three of them. Each has about twenty men. There are a few hundred warriors still attached to the estate and they are mostly undecided. They don't think the land should be split up and they are loyal to my father's memory. But I am not yet a man and they are not used to the idea of serving a woman. However, around here everyone worships the deer god and would do whatever he says."

Shika drew the Burnt Twins aside. "What should we do?" he asked quietly.

"People obviously know we are here," Nagatomo said.

"Sooner or later they will learn who you are. Either we move on now, farther north, or we take advantage of this new situation."

"It's an opportunity to stamp your mark here," Eisei added. "If you have allies and men in the Snow Country, you will return to Miyako with the east protected."

They both spoke of the future, Shika thought, whereas he still did not consider he had a future. One action would lead to another if he started to reengage with the world.

Tan, who had been following them through the forest at his own speed, trotted up to them, sniffing curiously at Takauji.

"What a fine horse," the boy exclaimed.

"What should I do, Lord Kiyoyori?" Shika said.

Tan pawed the ground and neighed shrilly. Naturally, Lord Kiyoyori wanted to fight.

"We should talk to your mother," Shika said to Takauji. "Where can we meet?"

Takauji pointed to a small shrine hut at the farther side of the lake, half-obscured by willow trees and hazel bushes. It had the high, steep roof of Snow Country buildings. Above its door, antlers had been fastened, some of the largest Shika had ever seen, and newly tanned deer hides were spread over the small veranda. A frayed and knotted rope hung beneath a wooden bell. "I will bring her there at this time tomorrow."

"We will be there," Shika promised.

"Can I touch your antlers?" Takauji asked.

Shika lowered his head. Takauji grasped the unbroken

branch and pulled sharply, jerking Shika forward, unbalancing him.

Shika cuffed him. "I told you, the mask does not come off."

"You really are the deer god, aren't you?" Takauji said, with awe.

*

When they returned to the forest hut and told Ibara what they had learned, she said, "I would like to do something to help Lord Takaakira's son, and his wife—she has suffered a lot in her life, I think."

"She must have seen very little of him," Eisei remarked.

"Yet he trusted her to run that vast estate in his absence," Ibara said. "She is by no means a helpless woman; it may be some kind of trap. Let me go first tomorrow. I should be sorry to die before Masachika, but apart from that my life is unimportant."

Shika smiled, though he knew no one could see it beneath the mask. "We could argue all night over whose life matters the least."

"I don't believe either of us has yet fulfilled our destiny," she replied in a low voice.

"Then you and I will go to the shrine and meet her together and give Heaven a chance to prove you are right. Nagatomo and Eisei will keep watch outside."

They rose early and were on the edge of the forest, with a clear view of the shrine, just after daybreak. They had hidden the horses farther back among the trees, but

Tan had followed them, picking his way carefully among the winter's dead leaves, through which blades of grass and flower stems were emerging. Under rocks the last of the snow still lingered. Gen walked stiff-legged behind Shika, turning his head to favor his right ear, now and then stopping to sniff the air.

Shika settled into a meditation position, Jato on the ground beside him, his bow on his back, while Eisei and Nagatomo checked that the shrine was empty. They then melted back into the forest.

Gen crouched on his haunches, a little in front. After some time, when the sun had burned the mist from the fields, the fake wolf raised his head and gave a faint whine. A few moments later, Shika heard the muffled tread of hoofs in the soft earth; only one horse, he thought.

A crow called: Nagatomo had heard the horse, too. A real crow replied from a tree nearby, making Shika grin.

The three figures came into sight, the woman riding, the boy running alongside. It was the same pony from the day before. It caught Tan's scent and stared toward the forest, whinnying a greeting. The other horses would have neighed back, had they been within earshot, but Tan remained silent.

The woman did not really ride the pony but rather used it as a method of transport. She had no other interest in it. He guessed she did not ride often. It stopped abruptly not far from the shrine and she slid from its back, as though thankful to get off.

The pony looked thankful, too, shook itself vigorously, and began to crop the new grass. The boy ran to the shrine, his knife drawn, and entered cautiously. After a few moments, he came out and beckoned to his mother.

She looked around once, took some offerings from a cloth, and went forward to place them on the steps. The boy pulled the bell rope and the wooden clapper gave out a hollow, eerie sound that made Shika's neck prickle. Gen gave a muffled howl.

Shika picked up his weapons and approached the shrine. Ibara emerged from the dead bracken where she had been concealed, and followed him. At the steps she touched his arm and indicated that she should go first, but at that moment Takauji appeared on the threshold and gestured to them to come in. Bending his head, Shika stepped inside.

For a moment he could see nothing in the gloom. He heard her gasp and could only imagine how the antlered mask had startled her. He made no bow or greeting, but she dropped to her knees, laid her palms flat on the floor, and lowered her head.

"My son told me," she whispered.

"I am not the deer god," he answered. "I am a man under enchantment, a curse, you could say."

"It must make you powerful," she said, more loudly, sitting up and gazing at him frankly. "Yes, I can see it does. Believe me, I know all about power."

He could see, now, the planes of her face, sharp features, pale, northern skin. There was something bird-like about her; she reminded him of a falcon, fierce and swift. Her hands and feet were very small, her wrists slender.

"Are you better with the bow or the sword?" she said, wasting no time.

"I believe I can outfight most men with both," he said, "but probably the bow suits me more."

She said, "I am glad of that. This is my plan. I don't want to plunge the whole of the Snow Country into war, brothers against brothers, fathers against sons, but until those who challenge me are dead, that war cannot be avoided. I am going to invite my husband's cousins to an archery contest, in honor of the deer god, and you will kill them."

She gave a thin-lipped smile. "Of course, there is no reason why you should help me. I don't know who you are or where you have come from."

"There are bonds between us," Shika replied. "My companion was employed by your late husband."

"Were you there when he died?" the lady said, turning her piercing eyes toward Ibara.

"No, lady."

"Are you a woman?" her voice was bitter. "Is that why you found *employment* with him?"

"No," Ibara said simply, and then, "I worked in his household."

"Looking after Kiyoyori's daughter, I suppose. I heard all about it. What a foolish thing to die for, don't you think? I will never forgive him, but I will never forgive Aritomo either." She was twisting her hands together, and then struck one fist with the other palm, and held her hands firmly so they would not move. "I'm sorry," she said. "It has become a habit, since I had the news of his death. What happened to the girl? I hope she is dead, too. It was an evil day when Takaakira came upon her."

"She drowned while trying to escape," Ibara said, levelly.

"So much the better. But you are a strange one! Dressed as a man, carrying a sword. What are you trying to achieve?"

Ibara gave Shika a look, and stepped to the open door, where she crouched down, staring at the lake.

"I have offended her . . . him . . . which should I say? I did not mean to talk about these things. Now I am upset."

Shika could see that her life had made her selfish and angry. He was inclined to leave her to it: let the relatives divide the estate as they desired. But Takauji interested him and he wanted to spare the boy the sort of childhood he himself had had.

She studied him as though divining his thoughts and said, "I suppose Aritomo would be very interested in knowing about you."

"He already knows about me," Shika said. "He has nightmares about me."

"Does he know that you are here, in the Snow Country?"

"By the time he learns that, I will be somewhere else." Her gall in trying to threaten him, in this oblique way, made him laugh.

She had the grace to look uncomfortable. "Well, as I said, I am no friend of the Minatogura lord. He will not hear about you from me. My men deeply resent their lord's death. They are Snow Country people. They know how to keep silent."

She got to her feet and came close to him. For a moment he thought she was going to touch the mask, and he wondered briefly if it would come off under her fingers, but though she looked at it intently, she did not reach out. She lowered her eyes to his legs, as though appraising him, making him aware that her husband had been dead for many months, and even before that she had been more or less abandoned. He felt her hawk-like determination. He admired her, but he did not in any way desire her.

✳

At night, it was still cold, and sometimes there were new falls of snow, but once the equinox had passed, spring came with a rush. In the days before the competition, targets made of bundles of straw, shaped like wild boar, with large painted eyes and real tusks, were set up along the lakeshore. Horses were washed and groomed, their winter coats brushed out, their manes and tails plaited with red. They caught the excitement and neighed wildly, stamping their feet and tossing their heads. From the marshes, nesting birds shrieked in response.

Takauji and his mother were given the place of honor on the steps of the shrine. All day men competed in heats, galloping past the targets and losing their arrows. The boar's eyes were considered the winning shot. Finally there were four rivals left, the three cousins and one of Lady Yukikuni's men, middle-aged, skillful and cunning, with a clever, nimble horse. None of them had achieved the perfect score of three eyes in a row.

As they were preparing to ride off against one another, the lady said in a clear voice, "There is one more competitor, the representative of the deer god himself. Who dares take him on?"

She beckoned to Shika and called, "Come out!"

Nyorin stepped out of the forest, his silver coat gleaming, his long mane decorated with flowers and leaves. A cry of surprise and awe came from the watching crowd. The other competitors fell back as the horse approached the shrine. Shika bowed his antlered head to the lady and her son and took the huge bow from his shoulder. Nyorin's nostrils flared and he uttered a challenging neigh as Shika turned him toward the starting point, breaking into a swift gallop as Shika dropped the reins on his neck and drew from his quiver one of the arrows he had made in the forest.

It was easy for him, far easier than shooting the werehawk from the sky. One after another, three arrows slammed into the boars' eyes.

Nyorin came to a halt and trotted back to the starting line, where he stood snorting in triumph as though saying, *Beat that!*

Shika was about to dismount and go to the lady when one of the cousins rode toward him, shouting, "Take off that mask and let us see who you really are!"

Several tried to dissuade him, but he had already drawn his sword and was thrusting toward Shika. Nyorin moved like lightning, striking out with his forefeet, giving Shika time to draw Jato.

The lady said in a clear voice, "He has drawn his sword against the deer god. Let him die."

No one saw who loosed the shaft that pierced the man's chest. It came out of the forest. Shika knew it was Nagatomo's. Within moments the other two cousins were dead. *Eisei and Ibara*, he thought. The straw boars stared with their blind eyes as the blood soaked into mud and sand.

The lady was on her feet, her pale face flushed with triumph. "It is the judgment of the forest itself!" she cried.

People drew back as Shikanoko rode away, afraid his shadow would fall on them.

※

The next day there were offerings on the edge of the forest, and every day after that. A week went by before the lady came, riding the dun pony, with Takauji leading it. She had brought Shika a pair of chaps made from wolf skins. The fur was gray and white, the bushy tails still attached.

After she had given them to him she said, "Stay with me as my husband. I know you are a man."

"If you can remove the mask, I will," he replied, not believing she could.

She smiled and reached out immediately, certain she

would succeed, but she could not shift it from his face. Tears of disappointment came to her eyes.

"Stay anyway," she begged. "I will tell no one. You may hide out in the forest all summer and I will come to you at night. You have seen how the farmers are already bringing you food. You will lack nothing. I will show you my gratitude."

Shika thanked her, but, as soon as she had left, without even any discussion among them, they prepared the horses, packed up their few possessions, and began to ride to the north.

5

KIKU

Once they had struck the northern coast highway and turned to the west, the three boys, Chika, Kiku, and Kuro, came across many other travelers: merchants with trains of packhorses; monks carrying stout sticks and begging bowls; officials and their retinues; warriors on horseback, in groups of three or four, offering their swords and their services as bodyguards; beggars, and probably not a few thieves, Chika thought, taking care to keep the treasure well hidden. They had divided it into three and put it into separate bags, though Kiku and Kuro had each taken a strand of pearl prayer beads to string around his neck. Kiku's entangled with the beak and talons of the werehawk.

Chika explained who all these people were, as best he could, adding to the knowledge Kiku and Kuro had acquired in their previous forays into the human world, but their grasp of how everything hung together was still flimsy.

"Is this the mountain where Akuzenji was king?" Kuro asked as they climbed up to the pass. The road was steep, hardly more than a track. Horses stumbled over rocks and slipped on the scree. Even high in the mountains, it was hot. Sweat dripped from men's faces, and the animals' bellies and legs were flecked with white stains.

"I suppose so, and this must have been the most dangerous part of the journey," Chika said. "Any number of men could lie hidden behind the outcrops, and there is nowhere to escape to."

The mountain rose steep and jagged on one side, and, on the other, the valley fell away, a sheer drop of hundreds of feet.

"That's where Akuzenji used to throw the bodies of those who refused to pay him," said a man who had been walking just behind them, leading a small horse laden with baskets. "Only they were not strictly speaking bodies, not until they reached the bottom, that is."

Kuro's eyes brightened with interest.

"Where are you boys walking to?" the stranger went on.

"Kitakami," Chika said.

"All alone? No family?"

Chika said warily, "In Kitakami—we are going to a relative's house."

"What is their name? I know most people in Kitakami."

"I don't remember."

"So where do they live?"

"Near the port," Chika improvised.

The man laughed. "In Kitakami everyone lives near the port. Well, if you find them, tell them Sansaburo from Asano says good day. May your journey be safe!"

He clicked his tongue at the horse and walked past them.

"What did he mean by all that?" Kiku said.

"I think he was just being friendly," Chika replied.

Kiku looked at Kuro, who raised his eyebrows as if he, also, did not understand.

At the top of the pass, they paused to catch their breath. The black cone of Kuroyama rose behind them, and in front lay fold after fold of ranges all the way to the west. In the distance, to the north, Chika could see the glimmer of the sea, and in the south a huge lake—Kasumi, he supposed. It was approaching evening; most travelers had hastened on to find lodging before dark. Only the friendly merchant was still on the road ahead of them.

Kiku, deep in thought, hardly looked at the view but, as they began the descent, said to Kuro, "Let's take that horse."

"All right," Kuro replied agreeably. "Shall I use the sparrow bee?"

"That'll do," said Kiku.

They quickened their pace until they had almost caught up with the man. Kuro took the cover from the wicker cage and the sparrow bee began to buzz angrily. He released the catch and the bee shot out, soaring briefly, then descending to attack. The man called Sansaburo from Asano gave a cry and danced around, waving his arms futilely. The bee stung him on both hands, then on the neck. Within moments he was lying in the dust, clutching at his throat.

"What have you done?" Chika cried in shock.

Kuro had grabbed the lead rope of the startled horse and was trying to catch the bee before it stung the horse, too. When he had succeeded he said, "Let's throw him over the edge."

"No, we'll leave him here," Kiku said.

"You killed him!" Chika said. "He'd done nothing to you!"

"Don't worry. I have a plan. We'll take the horse."

"What's in the baskets?" Kuro said, curious.

They loosened the well-tied knots on one of the baskets and prized open the lid. A faint fishy smell floated out.

"Just old shells?" Kiku said. "What use are they?"

Chika slipped his hand in among the shells and felt their smooth interiors. "It must be mother-of-pearl. It's used as decoration, in inlays and so on."

"Is it valuable?" Kiku asked.

"Very," Chika replied.

"We'll take it to the . . . who should we hand it over to?"

"What do you mean?" Chika asked.

"Aren't we going to keep it?" Kuro said.

"We must give it back," Kiku declared. "We'll say we found the horse, straying. But first we need to kill a couple more merchants, so people begin to be frightened."

Chika said doubtfully, "We'll be caught."

"I promise you, we will never be caught," Kiku said, with conviction. "Just tell me who we should take the shells to."

"I suppose to whoever ordered them. This man prob-ably took them to the same person, year after year."

"Hmm. I should have asked him that, before he died," Kiku said. "There's so much to learn. Well, you can make inquiries when we get to Kitakami."

They walked a little farther and, when night fell, went off the track into the forest to rest for a while. Kuro sat by the horse, keeping watch, and Chika and Kiku lay down, side by side. Kiku seemed to fall asleep immedi-ately, but Chika was wakeful, and when he did finally sleep he had a nightmare that one of Kuro's snakes was slithering toward him. He tried to run, but his limbs were paralyzed. The snake hissed and flickered its tongue and he knew that at any moment it would bite him and he would die. He woke to find Kiku's arms around him.

"You were screaming. What's wrong?"

"I had a bad dream."

Kiku said, sounding surprised, "It feels nice, holding you like this."

Chika lay without moving, letting the other boy touch him with exploring hands. He felt his body begin to respond to the pleasure. Their limbs entwined, their mouths joined, as they took the first steps on the journey of sex and death that would bind them to each other.

The second merchant was garroted by an invisible Kiku. They took his horse, loaded this time with bam-boo scoops and bowls. Kuro looked after the horses while Chika and Kiku fell on each other with the ferocious lust of young males, incited by their seeming power over life and death.

"Can you kill anyone you choose?" Chika asked, as he lay panting and exhausted.

"I don't know yet. I am finding out. It's fun, isn't it? The killing, and then this afterward? I had no idea it was all so much fun. I don't understand why people don't do it all the time."

"Some do," Chika replied. "But it's not so much fun for the people who die."

"If people did not die, there would be no room for new ones. And don't they just get reborn into a new life, anyway?"

They had heard monks and priests expounding the doctrine along the road.

"Can *you* be killed?" Chika asked, a new fear seizing him.

"I suppose so. Our fathers are mostly dead, and our mother." Kiku did not want to dwell on the subject. "So who shall we kill next? You choose."

The idea seemed suddenly irresistible, yet a few months ago it would have appalled him. His warrior upbringing was being corrupted and tainted by Kiku. He tried not to think of his father's stern teachings. He knew he was enthralled by Kiku, as by no one else in the world. He wanted to please him; he could not resist him.

"I bet you cannot kill a warrior," he challenged.

❋

He was not much of a warrior, a solitary, grizzled man with only one eye, the empty socket yawning disconcertingly. He sang ballads in a monotonous, melancholy voice outside a lodging place not far from Kitakami. Chika and Kiku watched him while the horses rested and drank and Kuro procured food. Chika found the strains of his voice, in the summer evening, curiously moving. He wondered where he had come from, what had reduced him to this.

He wore a faded green hunting robe and under it a corselet, missing much of its silk lacing; at his hip was a long sword. He did not earn enough for a meal, let alone a room, and began to walk away, his measured gait and the set of his shoulders indicating he was resigned to another night on the road.

The two boys sauntered after him, and Kuro pulled the reluctant horses along behind them. Kiku waved at his brother to fall back out of sight.

"Attract your warrior's attention," he whispered to Chika. "I'll grab him from behind and then you can use your sword."

Chika watched, with all the shock and thrill it always gave him, as Kiku faded into nothingness, and then, hastening his steps, called, "Hey, sir, wait a minute!"

The man turned. The sunset behind him made him appear solid, black and featureless, and for a moment Chika felt afraid, but as he came closer he saw the lines in the face and the gray hair. The remaining eye was clouded, two fingers were missing from the left hand. When the man finally moved, it was stiffly—no doubt he was troubled by old wounds.

"What do you want, boy?"

"I am traveling alone. I thought we could walk together."

The warrior gave him a shrewd look. "What happened to your companions and the horses?"

Chika said, "They have gone their own way. Maybe they stopped for the night."

"You carry a sword; you look like a warrior's son. Were you not taught to speak the truth, at all times?" His tone was forbearing, but the words flicked Chika like a whip.

"You are an expert on the life of a warrior, are you, you beggar?"

The man turned. "Walk by yourself. I am a little fussy in my choice of companions. If you ever learn any manners, you can approach me again."

Chika's hand was on his sword. At the same moment the warrior drew his own, turned as fast as a snake, and struck out.

Kiku gave a shriek, breaking into sight, grasping his arm, blood beginning to drip from it.

"What are you?" the warrior cried. "Forgive me, you should not sneak up on a man like that. It's instinctive, you see. I can't help but react. Now I have cut you!" His eyes went back to Chika's sword. "What? You were intending to kill me? Two shabby boys like you? You must be desperate! I have nothing but these clothes and my sword. I'll die before I hand that over!"

"I'm bleeding," Kiku said.

"It's not fatal," the man assured him. "Unless you are unlucky enough to get wound fever. Wash it well, that's my advice. And now, my young friends, unless the warrior's son wants to fight me, I'll be on my way."

"Wait," Kiku said. His brow was taut with pain and concentration. "What are you planning to do in Kitakami?"

"None of your business, brat."

"You must be hoping to find someone who can feed you, someone you can serve."

The warrior laughed. "And if I am, what's it to you?"

"How would you feel about serving me?"

He laughed again but more bitterly. "The first requirement of anyone I serve is that they be rich!"

"We are rich," Kiku said, pulling out the pearl prayer beads and fingering them. "But we don't know what to do in Kitakami and we are afraid of being cheated. We found these horses, wandering. We want to take them to their rightful owners. Not for any reward, we don't actually need it. Just to do the right thing."

Kiku had been turning paler and paler while he talked, and now he swayed as if he was about to faint.

The warrior sheathed his sword. "Come, let me take a look at that cut."

Chika knew he had a chance of killing him now, while he was unprepared. He saw the exact place in the neck where his blade would open the flesh and the blood vessels within. His hand flexed and clenched, his sword quivered. He was not sure if Kiku's faintness was a ploy to get the man off his guard.

"Put the sword away," the man said. "I may be one-eyed and crippled, but you still wouldn't stand a chance against me. Here," he tore a strip from his underrobe. "Run to the spring and wet this. We'll bind his arm."

"What is your name?" Chika asked after the wound was bound and Kuro and the horses had caught up with them.

"Yamanaka no Tsunetomo. And yours?"

"Kuromori no Motochika." He used his adult name.

"Huh? Everyone at Kuromori was slaughtered. So why are you still alive?"

"That's my business," Chika said, making Tsunetomo laugh.

"That's right, my friend. Some of us are called to die and some to survive at any price. If that's your path, embrace it, without regret or shame."

"Has it been your path?" Chika asked.

"Maybe it has," Tsunetomo said. "At any rate, I am still alive. Now, let's see what those horses are carrying."

It was almost dark, a warm night with no moon, the starlight diffused by the hazy air. Kuro made a fire and unloaded the baskets from the horses' backs. Tsunetomo inspected the contents.

"You found the horses straying, you say?"

Kiku nodded. His eyes were a little brighter in the firelight and his cheeks were flushed, but he no longer seemed faint, nor otherwise affected by the wound.

"What happened to the owners, I wonder?" Tsunetomo's face was expressionless, his voice bland.

"No sign of them," Kiku said.

"Maybe someone murdered them?" Kuro suggested.

"That's what people are saying," said Tsunetomo. "I've

already heard one or two rumors—Akuzenji's ghost, or some new bandit chief, or ogres who kill people to eat them. If such rumors continue to spread, more people will become afraid and soon no one will want to travel alone."

"That's good," Kiku said. "We can offer them protection—you and your sword."

"Am I to guard the whole length of the highway?" Tsunetomo laughed.

"You must know other people you can hire to help you."

"As a matter of fact, I do."

"So will you serve me?" Kiku asked.

Tsunetomo stared at him. "I will," he said finally. "You're a strange creature, but there's something about you . . . keep me in food and shelter, and a little extra for wine, and my sword is yours."

6

ARITOMO

The fiery death of the Prince Abbot had not only shocked and grieved Lord Aritomo but had also alarmed him. His hold on power was weakened, his authority shaken. With his usual clear-sightedness he knew it would take only one more blow to dislodge him. He strengthened the capital's defenses, while making plans to retreat to Minatogura, preparing boats at Akashi, in case attacks came from Shikanoko in the east and the Kakizuki in the west.

But his enemies did not take advantage of his momentary weakness. Shikanoko vanished into the Darkwood, Lord Keita and his retinue made no move from Rakuhara. Within a few weeks Masachika, whom Aritomo came to depend on even though he could not forgive him for Takaakira's death and some days could hardly bear to look at him, finally captured Kuromori and went on to take Kumayama. The east was once more secure.

Hoping to placate the vengeful spirit of the Prince Abbot, Aritomo gave orders for Ryusonji to be rebuilt, exactly as before, and for the dragon child to be worshipped there, yet the construction progressed slowly. After a series of inexplicable accidents, the carpenters refused to work, saying the place was occupied by ghosts and untethered spirits whom no one could control now that their master was gone.

The Imperial Palace, which had burned to the ground in the Ninpei rebellion, was also being rebuilt. In the meantime the Emperor, Daigen, and his mother were living in a nearby temple. The treasures that had been destroyed were slowly being replaced, but expenses were high and even Aritomo's new taxation system could not produce enough revenue. It was his custom to visit Daigen weekly, to take part in the rituals that bound Heaven and Earth through the sacred person of the Emperor. Daigen had been the Prince Abbot's choice and Aritomo could not fault him. He was intelligent, courteous, and, most important, biddable, seemingly resigned to his role as a figurehead and happy to play it in return for beautiful companions, wine, and poetry. There was no reason for harmony not to be restored, but, as the years passed, the drought worsened; rain hardly fell, the lake shrank and the river dried up.

Aritomo tried to wipe Takaakira's dying words from his mind: *Yoshimori is the true emperor.* Yet they haunted his dreams and he often woke suddenly in the night hearing a ghostly voice speak them in the empty room.

On one of his visits the Emperor's mother sent a

message through a courtier that she wanted to speak to him. He had to obey, yet he went with reluctance, fearing she was going to grumble about their living conditions or demand some new luxury for which he would have to find the money.

Lady Natsue received him alone. He prostrated himself before her, as was required, feeling a twinge of pain in his hips, regretting his sedentary life, longing for a horse beneath him, a hawk above, the brisk air and huge skies of the east.

It was a warm spring day and water trickled through the garden. The room was not unpleasant; it faced south and was elegantly appointed with flowing silk hangings and a few exquisite pieces of lacquered furniture. He could not see what she had to complain about.

"Please sit up, lord," Lady Natsue said.

He dared to look directly at her. She had been the late emperor's second wife, always, it was whispered, jealous of the first, Momozono's mother. Yet surely no one could have surpassed her in beauty. Even now, in apparent middle age, she seemed perfect, still youthful. She spoke at length about the joys of the season and the various flowers and birds of the garden, then told an amusing anecdote about a court lady and a mouse, which His Majesty had turned into a poem. When she fell silent he said, half-irritated, half-charmed, "What can I do for Your Majesty?"

"I need to speak to you about Ryusonji." She gestured that he should come nearer. The tone of her voice changed though it was no less attractive. "My late brother and I were very close," she whispered. "He shared many of his secrets with me. Under his rule Ryusonji became a place of great power. Now he is gone it lies empty; its power leaks from it."

"I am trying to rebuild it," Aritomo replied. "But the work is proving difficult and slow. No one can replace the Prince Abbot."

"I had heard about the problems. Last week I went to see for myself. I wanted to prepare for the anniversary of my brother's death, pay my respects and mourn him. Women, as you know, are not usually permitted to enter into spiritual mysteries, yet my brother recognized that in me dwelled an ancient soul that had acquired great wisdom. He often sought my advice and he promised me that if he died before me he would attempt to reach me from the other world. When I knelt before the half-completed altar I felt him call to me. He wants me to move into Ryusonji. I will be able to ensure that the re-pairs progress smoothly and the various disruptive spir-its are appeased. My son will come with me. It is fitting that the Emperor should be in the spiritual heart of his capital."

"I am not at all sure that it is fitting," Aritomo said, wanting to speak with his customary frankness yet fearing to offend her. "How shall I put it? The events that took place there, the deaths, the dark forces un-leashed . . ."

"I can handle any darkness at Ryusonji. The shadows are a source of power just as much as the light. When the new palace is finished maybe my son can live there.

But it is imperative that I move quickly, for someone else is about to take possession of the temple."

"What do you mean?" Ever since he had been told of the details of the confrontation between the Prince Abbot and Shikanoko, he had had nightmares in which a masked half-human figure confronted him in judgment. Now the Empress's words summoned up that image. He feared it was what he would find at Ryusonji. Yet Shikanoko was surely far away, in the Darkwood.

"An old man is there, camped out in one of the cloisters. He plays the lute and sings. I was told he was harmless, wandering in his mind, but his presence seemed offensive so I ordered him to be removed. However, no matter how many times he was thrown out, he always returned. Finally the guards lost patience with him and beat him to death, they thought, but the next day they heard the lute and his voice——he was back in the cloister. Now no one dares approach him. I believe I know what he is doing there. He has obtained the Book of the Future and means to erase my son's name and inscribe that of Yoshimori."

Neither of them spoke for a moment. The trickling of the stream seemed suddenly louder and birds called from the garden.

"Who is he?" Aritomo whispered.

"The monks who survived told me he is Sesshin, once many years ago a fellow student of my brother. He became a great master who gave his power away to the evil man they call Shikanoko."

"Gave his power away?" His skin was crawling. He

had heard of Sesshin before, some connection with Matsutani and Masachika. And then he remembered, and the terrible day Takaakira died came back to him.

"So he could pass as a foolish old man," Lady Natsue explained. "But little by little he is gathering knowledge again. He has all the time in the world since he has made himself immortal."

He stared at her in disbelief, wondering if he had misheard.

She repeated the word, "Immortal."

"What is his secret?" Aritomo said hoarsely.

"That interests you, Lord Aritomo?" Her gaze pierced him. "Would you steal it from him? Would you wish never to die?"

"I want more time," he replied. "I don't want to die before I have achieved all I strive for."

"None of us can know the hour of our death," she said, her eyes not leaving his face. "The water from the well at Ryusonji is reputed to prolong life. My brother and I have both drunk from it. I am much older than you think, but I am still as mortal as my brother proved to be."

The wind had risen and leaves rustled from outside, a branch scraping against the roof. A crow called harshly as if it were sitting directly above them. He felt parched, almost feverish. Surely it was hotter than it should be?

"Lord Aritomo," she said. "Are you unwell?"

"No!" he replied, his voice suddenly loud. He was never sick; he denied illness access to his body. Even battle blows glanced off him, hardly leaving a wound. But the idea of an immortal at Ryusonji, slowly rewriting the Book of the Future, had struck deeply inside him. He struggled to regain calm.

"I will inspect Ryusonji myself," he said. "If I consider it suitable you and His Imperial Majesty may move there."

"Let us not waste any more time." Lady Natsue inclined her head graciously.

※

When Aritomo returned to his own palace, the one abandoned by Lord Keita when the Kakizuki fled from the capital, he sent for Masachika, who, he knew, had just come back from Minatogura. It was not long before the Matsutani lord was kneeling in front of him, apparently in perfect submission. Aritomo studied him for a few moments. Masachika was undeniably a handsome man, and he had gained great popularity and respect since the discovery and capture of the Autumn Princess, but Aritomo thought he could read his deeper character clearly, seeing how opportunistic and self-serving all his actions and words were. He did not trust his loyalty, yet, though he did not like admitting it, Masachika had made himself indispensable.

First he told Masachika of the Empress's request and asked him to inspect the temple and make all necessary preparations.

"I will come with you. I have not visited Ryusonji myself since the Prince Abbot died. But what news do you bring from the east? I hope you have sorted out your personal life."

Masachika smiled, a little embarrassed. "I finally convinced Keisaku and his daughter that I was never going to marry her. I could have taken her as a second wife, but I did not want to distress Lady Tama, after all she has suffered. I found a suitable husband for the young woman, and released Keisaku from all obligations to me. They will hold Keisaku's estate in vassalage to you, which protects Minatogura from the north. It seemed an acceptable solution all around, provided Lord Aritomo agrees, of course."

"It will be good to have someone loyal in between the port and the Snow Country. I had hoped Takauji would be removed. I cannot trust him not to challenge me sooner or later. But I hear the cousins failed in their efforts to get rid of him?"

"Yes, and they are all dead now. The mother arranged an archery contest. An unknown archer, who she claimed was the deer god, came out of the forest to win it, and the challengers were all killed. She said it was the judgment of the forest. Takauji is, unfortunately, more secure than ever."

When Aritomo made no response Masachika said, "He is the son of the man who betrayed you. You cannot trust him."

"I am fully aware of that," Aritomo snapped, enraged that Masachika should speak so of Takaakira, who had been so superior to him in every way. Yet he knew he was right. Unless he was removed, Takauji would be a continuing threat. "I cannot deal with him now," he said, more calmly. "First we must destroy the Kakizuki. Did you find out the identity of this so-called deer god?"

Masachika said, "All the evidence—the antlered mask, the skill with the bow, the fake wolflike creature— suggests it was Shikanoko."

Aritomo kept his face still, his expression impassive, yet a kind of dread was welling up in him.

Masachika went on. "By the time my men investigated he had disappeared again. The archery contest took place weeks ago. Shikanoko could be anywhere by now. Takauji was extremely hostile and my men were lucky to return alive. Unlike those I sent immediately after the disaster at Ryusonji, who never came back. Remember, we are not dealing with an ordinary fugitive but with a sorcerer."

"Is it his power that makes the rain dry up? How do I combat that? I don't mind facing a thousand men on a battlefield, but this one sorcerer keeps evading me."

"Shikanoko has no men, no army," Masachika said. "All were destroyed at Kumayama. If he had been going to challenge you he would have done it immediately after the death of the Prince Abbot. I don't think he will ever emerge from the Darkwood. If you don't provoke a snake it will not bite you."

"Is he completely alone?"

"He has a few companions, I believe: the ones they call the Burnt Twins, one is a former monk from Ryusonji, the other from Kumayama, and one other whose name and identity I have not been able to discover."

"So some survived from Kumayama?"

"These were already with him. But there are always some survivors. Some hide, some run away, some are left for dead but recover from their wounds."

"I will never eradicate all my enemies," Aritomo said.

Masachika nodded in sympathy. "But we will do our best to control and weaken them. I did find out something else, probably not very important. One of the women left at Kumayama told me. Shikanoko's mother became a nun, after her husband, Shigetomo, died. Apparently she is still alive and is in a convent a little way from Aomizu, on Lake Kasumi."

"What would she know about anything? It must be years since she forsook the world."

"As I said, it's not likely to be important."

"Well, follow it up anyway," Aritomo said. "Arinori is in Aomizu now. He can look into it. There's no need to go yourself. Write a message."

Arinori had served him for years and had been rewarded with Lake Kasumi and the surrounding districts. He was an experienced seaman, ambitious and determined. Aritomo trusted him far more than Masachika, though he had to admit the latter was considerably more intelligent.

❋

The next day they rode in an ox carriage to Ryusonji. Both had dressed carefully and soberly in formal clothes, each with a small black hat on his head. A large retinue followed on horseback. Aritomo traveled frequently around the capital, inspecting new buildings and repairs, over-seeing merchants and craftsmen, keeping an eye out for excesses of luxury and extravagance that would attract new taxes to pay for horses, armor, and weapons.

People dropped to their knees as he went by, but he inspired fear, not love. The city ran smoothly, his offi-cials keeping every section meticulously administered, but neither he nor they could make the rains fall at their appointed time or save the crops when they failed.

The lake at Ryusonji had shrunk; the exposed bed was muddy and foul-smelling. A charred spiral of black across rocks and moss still showed where the burst of flame had scorched the ground and set fire to the build-ings. Most of the blackened beams had been removed and new lumber was stacked in the courtyards. There seemed to be some desultory activity, workmen sawing planks and preparing floors, but it was still far from finished.

"The Empress wants to move here as soon as possi-ble," he said to Masachika as they descended from the carriage. "See if there is anywhere suitable for tempo-rary lodging. If she is to be believed, her presence here will speed the completion."

Masachika went to speak to the head carpenter. Ari-tomo waited in the shade of the cloister, trying to sharpen all his senses, to discern what was really going on at Ryusonji.

The sound of a lute came to him, its mournful, plan-gent notes turning his spine cold. Masachika came back, saying enthusiastically, "This hall is nearly finished. It could be ready before the end of the month. I will start arranging furnishings and servants."

"They will need many rooms," Aritomo said. "And priests, guards, and so on. What happened to all the priests and monks who were here before?"

"Some died in the fire, I believe. The rest must have run away."

"Well, the Empress will bring her own, no doubt. Consult the steward of the Imperial Household."

Masachika inclined his head. "I will, lord."

If he resented being given this tedious, if prestigious, responsibility, he gave no sign of it. Aritomo knew he could rely on him, that Masachika would complete the task as swiftly and efficiently as he did everything. Yet, no matter how competent Masachika was, Aritomo would never warm to him.

The notes of the lute trickled through the air as if they were summoning him.

"Let us inspect the other courtyards," he said.

The sun beat down on the blindingly white stones, making his head ache. The new moss was an unnaturally brilliant green. The shadows under the cloisters were deep black.

The lute player sat cross-legged, the lute in his lap, his face turned to them as if he had been waiting for them.

Aritomo saw the hollow eye sockets, the shriveled lids.

Masachika exclaimed, "It is Master Sesshin!"

"The one whom your wife had blinded?"

"Yes, it was his eyes that I replaced at Matsutani and so subdued the guardian spirits."

"I remember," Aritomo said coldly. He could not take his eyes off the old man. So this was what immortality looked like! When the physical body could not die, did it simply mean endless pain and suffering? The deformed frailty before him tempted him briefly, savagely. He had often seen how under torture life persisted longer than he would have believed possible, but eventually it was extinguished. The Empress had told him the old man could not be killed and he wanted to put her claim to the test.

"Your lordship should not concern himself with the old lute player." The head carpenter had followed them into the courtyard and stood beside them, regarding Sesshin with an indulgent smile. "He is our talisman, aren't you, grandfather?"

He spoke in a loud voice and Sesshin nodded and smiled with senile glee.

"As long as he is left alone to play and sing, our work progresses. I bring him some food every day, not that he takes more than a mouthful. Since he returned there have been no accidents, no fires. The men say the dragon child must like his songs."

"Does he have any books?" Aritomo said, remembering what the Empress had said.

The workman shook his head. "I don't think so. What use would he have for books since he cannot see?"

Aritomo leaned over Sesshin and said loudly, "Where is the Book of the Future?"

"I will show it to you, one day," Sesshin replied, his voice low and rational. "And you will see whose name is written in it. There is no need to shout. I am not deaf."

Then he took up the lute and began to pluck the strings with his long fingernails.

"That's the way," the head carpenter said approvingly. "Keep playing for us!"

"I will come back and talk to him again," Aritomo said. There was so much he did not understand, it was unsettling him. The feeble old man who was somehow immortal, the Book of the Future: none of it made sense. And it was too hot, the wind was too dry. He longed for the gray skies and constant drizzle of the plum rains. He decided he would make sure the old man stayed here so he knew where he was, and he would come to question him, alone, and discover his secrets.

7

HINA (YAYOI)

Yayoi grew taller and, in her third spring at the temple, her body began to change. Her breasts swelled and she bled monthly, like all the women, attuned to the cycle of the moon. She had seen first Yuri, and then Asagao, become women in the same way—indeed, Asagao made sure there was not a single detail in the process that Yayoi did not know about—so she was not shocked or frightened as young girls sometimes were. Mostly she accepted womanhood—what else could she do?—but she also grieved for that girl child, single-minded and courageous, now gone forever.

Yuri left the temple one spring, making the journey on her own, the palanquin waiting at the foot of the steps. Sada and Sen, the two sisters, wept for days. Asagao was now the oldest girl. She did not sing them to sleep as Yuri had. She teased them for their red eyes and, when no one else was around, she bullied them. She left the

7

following year. Lady Fuji herself came for her, bringing another young girl, whom she entrusted to Yayoi's care.

"You, yourself, will be ready soon," she said with her familiar, appraising look.

The girls missed Asagao, her high spirits, her teasing ways. Even Sada and Sen wept for her, while Yayoi felt bereft, as though she had lost a limb.

In the sixth month of that year, when they had given up hoping for the plum rains, men came on horseback, demanding to speak to the Abbess. Their leader was obviously a warrior of high rank, though the nuns did not know him. He wore a crest of a sail above waves and the white stars of the Miboshi.

Men's voices, their heavy tread, their sweaty smell, were so unusual, it threw the girls and the nuns, even the ginger cat, into a state of anxiety and agitation. The men spoke politely, yet there was an undertone of menace. The lord made it clear that the women's temple survived only on his sufferance. One word from him and it would all be destroyed.

The Reverend Nun tried to hide the girls, but the men demanded to see every person living in the place. She rapidly tore off the robes they usually wore and made them put on nuns' habits and servants' clothes, rubbed dirt and ash on their faces and hands. They had never seen her so distressed and it alarmed them into silence.

Yayoi was terrified one of the men might be Masachika, her uncle. Would she even recognize the man who had killed Saburo in front of her eyes? Would he know her, after all these years? But all the men seemed strangers to her and, though they studied her intently, she did not think any of them knew her.

They did not lay hands on the girls, but they touched the older women, patting their breasts and feeling between their thighs, and one nun, taller than the others and somewhat masculine in look, was forced to disrobe to prove she was not a man.

Since the men hardly spoke, no one knew who or what they were looking for. They searched every corner of the temple, from the chests that held the sacred sutras to the woodpile stacked on the southern wall.

"Why did they spend so long at the fishpond?" Yayoi asked after they had left.

"People hide underwater," the Reverend Nun replied, "and breathe through hollow reeds—or so I have heard."

She helped the girls clean themselves, her hands shaking. "I suppose we were lucky. None of you has been harmed and nothing has been damaged that can't be mended."

Torn manuscripts, a broken statue, ripped hangings, a shattered ceiling, doors forced out of their tracks— the tall nun, weeping silently, set herself to repairing them.

Yayoi, now the oldest, undertook the task of calming and consoling the other girls. They all, like her, had fears from the past that had been reawakened by the armed men. She took out the lute and forced it to play soothing music, wondering where Yoshi was and if she and Genzo would ever be in his presence again. Several sutras needed recopying; Sada had quite a gift for writing, and she and Yayoi worked on them together, Yayoi reading them aloud.

When they were finished, she took them to the Abbess for her approval, kneeling quietly while the older woman read through them, reciting each syllable under her breath. Yayoi felt that peace was being restored with every precious word. Even the cat was calmed; she could hear its loud rhythmic purring.

The Abbess said suddenly, "They were looking for a man whom they called Shikanoko."

Yayoi felt shock run tingling through her limbs. Her heart thumped.

"I did not understand why they thought such a man, an enemy of Lord Aritomo, a warrior and a sorcerer, would be here at our insignificant temple. They told me they had recently discovered he was my son, and therefore there was every reason to suspect I was hiding him."

Yayoi said nothing, silenced by astonishment.

"My son, whom I have not seen since he was a young child, whom I believed to be dead. Not a day has passed that I have not prayed for him, but all my prayers, it seems, have gone unanswered. They say he has become a monster. He murdered his uncle through dark magic and then destroyed the Prince Abbot and the temple at Ryusonji. Now, these men say, Lord Aritomo believes it is his evil power that has cursed the realm and caused the rain to cease and the rivers to dry up. I told them if I knew where he was, I would have handed him over to them. But I do not know."

She stopped speaking and stood abruptly. The cat, alarmed, ran out of the room.

"And now our temple has come to the attention of Lord Aritomo. He sent Arinori to investigate me. I could tell Lord Arinori was shocked that we had no priests overseeing us. He asked how we ran our affairs and I was forced to reveal our benefactress, Lady Fuji. She will not thank me for that. No doubt she will come under his scrutiny next. They also inquired to whom we paid tax and I had to admit that we pay no tax to anyone." She went to the door and gazed out on the garden. "I cannot believe he has grown up to be so evil, but he had a fierce temper even as a baby. He screamed and bit my breasts. My women said that meant he would be a powerful warrior. But how did he fall into sorcery?"

Yayoi longed to reveal all she knew of Shikanoko, how he had served her father for a while, his kindness to her and her brother, the way he had cared for Sesshin after the old man had been blinded. She remembered the day he had arrived at Matsutani, riding Risu, the bad-tempered brown mare, and how he had been able to shoot down the werehawk that no one else could. But she did not dare open her mouth. Waves of emotion swept over her, so violent she feared she would faint. *What is this? What is wrong with me?*

"I must renew my prayers," the Abbess was saying. "I will fast for the next week, while I endeavor to restore tranquillity to myself and my temple. Let no one disturb me."

Through the next few weeks, Yayoi became aware

that what had been a childish fantasy about Shikanoko—
that she would grow up to marry him, cherish him, make
him smile, wipe the sorrow from his heart—had become
a true adult emotion. The knowledge sustained her. It
was a secret as precious as a sutra to be carried in her
heart, binding her spirit to his, in the same way the
sacred words bound the earthly and the divine.

Lady Fuji came unexpectedly at the beginning of
autumn. The typhoons had brought some rain, but less
than usual. Summer crops had been sparse, and the
shortage of food and the approach of winter had caused
unrest among the farmers. It was being harshly sup-
pressed, Lady Fuji told them, and Miboshi warriors were
everywhere.

"That is why I need you, Yayoi, my dear," she said,
with a sigh. "It is earlier than I planned, but only by six
months or so. And look at you, you are ready. Something
has awakened you."

The other girls wept bitterly and Yayoi could not
prevent tears forming in her own eyes. She went to bid
farewell to the Abbess and received back the text, the
Kudzu Vine Treasure Store, that Master Sesshin had
given her all those years ago.

"Let us read it together one last time," the older
woman said. "Really it is an honor that it has dwelled
with us all these years. It has blessed us and so have you."

Yayoi let the pages fall open where they willed.

The Abbess was studying her face. "What has it
shown you today?"

"It tells of a stone that reveals sickness," Yayoi said,

deciphering the faded gold letters on the indigo dyed page. "Here is a picture—but now it is gone again!"

It had given her a tantalizing glimpse: a surface of perfect smoothness, a dark mirror that had allowed her just one brief glance into its depths.

"Ah, I wonder," the Abbess murmured.

"What is it?" Yayoi asked.

"If you were staying here I would tell you, but there is no point now." The Abbess could not hide her distress. "How I will miss you! I deeply regret the path you are being forced to follow."

"I still don't understand the truth of the world and why there is so much pain!" Yayoi could feel tears threatening. She did not want to leave; she wanted to stay and learn more about the mysterious stone, but she knew the peace and seclusion of the temple were no more than an illusion. Ever since the Miboshi warriors had come to search for Shikanoko, none of the women had felt entirely safe.

"I will always pray for you," the Abbess continued.

"And I for you," Yayoi replied.

"Use what you find in the text only for healing. Do not follow my son into sorcery."

Yayoi bowed without speaking. *I would follow him even into the realms of hell*, she thought.

Fuji had brought a second palanquin with her. When Yayoi had arrived, she had been a child, small for her age. Now that she had reached her adult height she would no longer fit inside a palanquin with the other woman. But she also felt Fuji was glad to keep her distance, that she was not entirely comfortable with whatever plan she had for her. She did not look Yayoi in the eye or embrace her spontaneously as she had when she had come to collect Asagao. Alone in the palanquin, Yayoi had plenty of time to imagine what might be going to happen to her and to dread it.

It was dusk when they arrived at Aomizu and the boats on the dock were bright with red lanterns, the lights reflected in the still waters like a host of fireflies. The moon was a crescent in the sky, waxing toward its ninth-month fullness. Music was playing and Yayoi could hear singing. She thought she recognized Asagao's voice and was slightly comforted. She longed to see Take, and then thought of the boy called Yoshi, and felt the lute in her lap begin to stir.

One of the women whispered to Fuji as they stepped onto the boat. "He is here."

"What, already?" Fuji exclaimed, biting her lip. "We hardly have time to prepare her. Quick, bring some water. Let me wash her feet at least. How impatient these Miboshi are," she muttered as she brushed dust from Yayoi's robes and combed her hair until it fell silky and tangle-free down her back.

"Yayoi," she said, her voice serious and cold. "You are a clever girl, they tell me. You know what is expected of you. Charm this warrior, do whatever he wants, please him in every way. My future, the future of all of us on the boats, depends on it."

She led Yayoi to the stern of the boat where the bamboo blinds surrounded the largest of the separate spaces.

She dropped to her knees, raised the blind on one side, and, bowing to the ground, said, "My lord, I have brought the one you requested."

Yayoi found herself on her knees shuffling forward. The blind unrolled behind her with a slight rustle. The lanterns outside threw wavering shadows as the boat rocked slightly on the water of the lake.

A lamp burned in one corner, the scent of oil strong. By its light she saw him sitting cross-legged, a flask of wine and a bowl beside him. It was the lord, Arinori, who had come to the temple.

"Don't be afraid," he said. "Here, drink a little wine, it will relax you."

She took the bowl and sipped, the liquor flowing like fire into her throat and stomach. It did not relax her but had the opposite effect, making her heart pound with fear. Her whole being recoiled from the idea that this stranger, enemy even, should have intimate access to her body. How is it possible, she thought, that men have such power over women? That even Fuji was complicit in this transaction, which probably bought her privileges, which was pleasing to all parties except Yayoi herself, without whom the transaction would never have taken place?

"They could not really turn such a little pearl into a serving girl," he said, coming closer, putting his hand on the back of her neck, feeling her hair, pulling her face to his. His other hand was inside her robe, caressing her breast, and then reaching farther down, forcing her thighs apart.

He had the hard body, the iron muscles, of a warrior. He was nearly twice her size. When he thrust into her it was like being knifed. She could not help crying out from pain and fear. It excited him and she felt the gush of his release, alien in its smell and wetness.

Afterward he was kind to her, in a way. He stroked her hair and called her his little princess. He held the wine bowl close to her lips so she could drink, and kissed the tears from her eyes.

He wanted her to know he was a prize, how lucky she was to have attracted him. He was rich and powerful, he would always take care of her. Lord Aritomo himself had named him, he boasted. They were as close as brothers. That week he came every day, expressing his pleasure with gifts of silk robes, casks of wine, and the fine-quality rice that was otherwise almost impossible to obtain. Fuji was delighted and showered Yayoi with compliments and affection, any remorse she might have felt dispelled by the success of the transaction.

"Lord Arinori has become our protector. It is just as I hoped. But, Yayoi, you look so thin, you must not lose weight. Eat, eat, it's the sweetest rice we've had all year. Don't fret, don't dwell on what might have been. This is your life now and, while it may not be what your parents might have hoped for you or what you would have chosen, it is better than being dead. Enjoy it, strive to please Lord Arinori, and one day he may even buy you from me for his own."

Yayoi could not imagine anything worse. When Arinori's duties took him back to the capital, she began to choose men from the visitors that came aboard at Majima, Kasumiguchi, Kitakami, and the other market towns around the lake. She learned their desires and their foibles, their needs and their strengths. Some she liked more than others, some became almost friends. But not one of them ever knew that, when she embraced him and gave herself to him, in her heart it was not him she was holding but the wild boy who had ridden into her father's lands on a brown mare all those years ago.

8

MU

The fox girl laughed when Mu asked her name, as she laughed at most of his questions.

"You can call me Shida, if I have to have a name," she said, tickling him with a dried fern. She liked to drape herself in the leaves and flowers of the forest as they came into season, making garlands from strands of berries and the brown fronds of bracken for herself and Kaze, and for the child, when it came.

They had been together for four winters. The child was a girl, as slight and delicate as a fern leaf herself. They called her Kinpoge, after the celandines that starred the forest floor around the time of her birth. She did not seem to have any fox attributes, apart from her animal-like agility and her rapid growth, though in certain lights her thick hair had a russet gleam to it and her eyes were amber.

During those years, Shida taught Mu the bright playful magic of the fox people. It seemed to have no purpose other than to make life amusing. She cast a spell on Ban's skull, to Kaze's utter delight, that sent the horse flying through the air. She summoned up shape shifters, tanuki, cranes, turtles, and snakes, just for the fun of startling Ima or Ku. They never knew if an iron pot was really a pot or a grinning fat-bellied tanuki, or if an old robe, thrown on the ground, might not suddenly sprout wings and launch itself, squawking, into the air.

Her presence seemed to revive many of Shisoku's fake animals. One of the creatures, a cross between a dog and a wolf, which had been Shisoku's water carrier, raised its head from where it had fallen by the stream and Shida ran to help it to its feet, chuckling at its awkward gait.

"You should make a companion for it," she said, when it tried to lift the water vessel on its own and the water spilled out lopsidedly.

Mu had to admit he did not know how to and that all he did not know overwhelmed him. The forest and the mountain were home to thousands of plants, flowers, trees, and grasses, and myriad creatures, insects, birds, and small animals as well as deer, monkeys, foxes, bears, and wolves. There was no one who could teach him their names. Shida did not understand his need to label them. They were all instantly recognizable to her, she did not need words. Mu realized she lived like an animal, in each single moment, observing, feeling, enjoying, but not reflecting or recording. Sometimes he felt himself slipping into the same way of being, and days would pass when he hardly had a single thought. Then he would wake in the night from a bad dream in which a stranger who was at the same time familiar accused him of wasting his life. He would lie there in the dark, hearing the others breathing around him, alarmed and uneasy at what he was leaving undone, yet ignorant of what it might be.

He became preoccupied and silent. Shida accused him of being gloomy and turning into an old man before his time. There were no mirrors to look in; he could not check his appearance, yet he felt she was right. He was aging rapidly. He could see the same thing happening to Ima and Ku. Kaze grew like a human child, but the brothers seemed fated to have lives as short as insects'.

And as pointless, he thought.

Even before Kiku returned, Mu and his fox wife quarreled. Her playful magic no longer enchanted but irritated him. She began to spend time away, with her own people. He missed her with a kind of agony, but was angry with her when she came back.

And then one day Kiku rode into the clearing with Chika and an older man, a warrior with missing fingers and one eye.

They had an air of prosperity about them; their cheeks were fat and their hair sleek. The horses were sturdy, with bright eyes and round haunches. Mu saw the hut and the clearing through his brother's eyes and felt ashamed.

Kiku made no comment, hardly even greeted his

brothers, but said as he dismounted, "I have come for the skull."

"Do you remember where we buried it?" Mu said, thinking of the day when its owner, the monk, Gessho, had died.

"Oh, yes!" Kiku said.

"What will you do with it?" Mu asked.

Kiku cast a look at Ban, the horse skull he had tried to infuse with power, which stood on its post, motionless. "I know what I'm doing now. Our father, Akuzenji, had other sorcerers in his service. Tsunetomo took me to one who was familiar with these old matters. He taught me what I have to do. I'm going to try again."

"Ban can fly," Kaze told him. "Shida did it."

Kiku turned his gaze on Shida, who sat by the fire staring at him with frank interest. "You can do magic, Lady Shida?"

"A bit of this, a bit of that," she said carelessly. "Why do you call me *Lady*?"

"You're a beautiful woman. Are you my brother's wife?"

"No!" she said, laughing, even as Mu said, "Yes!"

Kiku said, "I need a beautiful woman to infuse the skull with power."

"Find your own wife," Mu said.

"I have come for my wife," Kiku replied. "I am going to take Kaze as my wife, sister of my dearest friend. Isn't that right, Chika?"

Chika nodded without speaking. Mu noticed he stayed by Kiku's side, as close as a dog.

Kiku went on, "But the ritual demands something different, some other woman, one more like our mother."

"If you touch her, I will kill you," Mu said.

"Don't be silly," said Shida. "You can't dictate what I can and can't do. I don't belong to you. If he wants me to join him in some magic, where's the harm in that?"

Kiku said to Chika, "Go and dig up the skull. Ima will show you where it is. Then boil a pot of water, Ima. We will clean it tonight, and tomorrow we will start the ritual."

"No!" Mu cried and leaped at his brother, not knowing what he intended to do, driven only by fear and frustration. But his arms were seized by the warrior, who up to this time had not spoken and who moved faster than Mu would have thought possible. He was strong, too, and held Mu with no effort. Mu struggled to use the second self, to turn invisible, but it was so long since he had used either that he was not quick enough.

"What shall I do with him?" the warrior asked.

"I don't know," Kiku said impatiently.

"Do you want me to kill him?"

"No, not really. I don't want him interfering or distracting me."

"He won't distract you if he's dead," the warrior said with a laugh, and tightened his grip on Mu's neck, as if he would break it with his bare hands.

"But it would be an inauspicious start to the rituals," Chika said. "Take him to the other side of the stream, Tsunetomo, and tie him up there."

Tsunetomo picked Mu up and strode across the

stream. Then, despite Mu's struggles, he trussed him like a goose, in a kneeling position, his hands tied to his feet behind his back. His knots were expert; there was no way Mu could wriggle out of the ropes. After an hour his joints and muscles had set up a scream of pain that dulled his hearing and his senses to everything else.

As night came, Ku brought water and stayed beside him, helping him to drink, whimpering like a dog.

"Untie me," Mu begged, unable to keep himself from whimpering, too.

"They say they will kill you if I do."

"I would rather be dead, for then I would not feel."

He could hear all night long the hiss and bubble of the water that was boiling the skull clean.

※

The rituals lasted for several days, during which time, as far as Mu could tell, Kiku and Shida were alone in the hut, with the skull. Every now and then he heard the others talking, smelled the food Ima and Kaze prepared—he himself refused to eat—and saw the horses come to the stream to drink. The sight of him alarmed them, as if they could not determine what he was, and they gazed at him with huge eyes and pricked ears. Often, a silence descended on the clearing, a sudden hush as if the whole forest held its breath in awe at what was taking place within the hut, the transformations that were occurring. Nothing, no one could help being affected by it. When sounds and voices returned, they were solemn and muted. Under Mu's tormented eyes, the hut seemed to glow with light, transformed into an enchanted palace in a garden of wisteria.

Kiku finally emerged and held the skull aloft. It was lacquered now and gleamed black and red with brilliant green jeweled eyes and cinnabar lips, the teeth inlaid with mother-of-pearl. Mu saw it clearly, because his brother brought it to the side of the stream to wave it in his face.

It was midday. The sun sparkled on the water, on the wet stones, on the mother-of-pearl.

They began to make preparations to leave. Mu heard Kiku's voice.

"Ku and Ima, you will come with me. From now on we must all be together. I have taken everything I need from this place, its treasure, its knowledge."

"What about Mu?" Ima said.

"He can stay here and become like Shisoku," Kiku replied.

"I'm not leaving the animals," Ku said stubbornly.

Kiku turned the skull toward him and went closer. "I am your older brother and you will obey me."

Ku tried to take a step back, but Kiku lowered the skull, grasped his arm, and forced him to stare into his eyes. Mu could not see what happened, but within seconds Ku had slumped to the ground.

"Pick him up and put him on your horse," Kiku ordered Tsunetomo, and the warrior obeyed, screwing up his face in a sort of unwilling admiration.

"Now you," Kiku addressed Ima, but Ima shook his head.

"I need to look after things here. I'll stay with Mu and Kinpoge."

Mu saw Kiku repeat the same process, and stare intently into Ima's eyes. But Ima stared back. Whatever power the skull had given Kiku did not work on him.

Kiku's eyes flashed with anger and for a moment Mu feared Tsunetomo would be ordered to kill them both. The warrior had his hand on his sword, as eager as a hunting dog.

Kiku turned to the horse, which Chika held ready for him. As he mounted, and Chika lifted Kaze up behind him, he said, "Stay, then. You can untie Mu now."

Mu screamed as the blood flowed back into his cramped legs. It was a long time before he could stand. When he finally managed it, on ankles that kept bending the wrong way beneath his weight, the clearing was empty, apart from Ima, and Kinpoge, who flitted around him like some ghostly spirit.

"Where is your mother?" he said to her, and her amber eyes filled with tears.

"She is in the hut," Ima said awkwardly. "I have tried to rouse her but . . ."

Mu hobbled slowly toward it, seeing it clearly in the afternoon light. The magic had all fled. It looked as dilapidated as usual, the roof sagging, the walls subsiding, revealing no trace of what had happened within it. He slid the door open and stepped in, his eyes adjusting to the dimness.

Shida lay on the ground, half-naked still, her legs apart, her arms above her head. He thought for a moment

had not been there, Mu and his daughter would have starved, or frozen to death, drifting into their long sleep without noticing. But Ima kept them both alive, going out daily to track hares or rabbits, occasionally bringing down, with an arrow, a squirrel or a pheasant, once even a serow, whose skin made a warm cape for Kinpoge. In some ways, hunting was easier, for against the white snow there was nowhere to hide and neither humans nor animals could conceal their tracks.

Ima kept the fire going, too, coming home with armfuls of dead wood, and cooked meals, roasting the tender joints, stewing the rest. Maybe it was the tempting smell of food, or Ima's tracks clear in the snow, that showed the tengu where they were.

The tengu came in the late afternoon, when a blood-red sun was sinking rapidly behind the western mountains, and it was already freezing. The light from the fire and from the lamps in the hut looked tiny against the great snowy mass that the Darkwood had become.

Kinpoge must have seen him first, lurking in the shadows just beyond the firelight, for she cried out and jumped into Ima's arms. Mu looked into the darkness and saw two red eyes glaring at them. He felt for the knife that Ima had been using to cut up the rabbit that would be their supper. Ima slid Kinpoge off his lap, pushed her behind him, and reached for his bow.

The tengu was dressed in bright blue leggings and a short red jacket. He had a long, beaklike nose, and when he sat down opposite Mu, he made a curious shrugging movement to adjust something feathery between his shoulders, which, at first, Mu thought was a dead bird and then realized was wings. The wings were grayish white and shaggy, almost indistinguishable from the tengu's thick shock of hair. He pulled out a sword and a bow, which he had been carrying on his back between the wings, and laid them down, the sword on his left, the bow on his right.

He gave Mu a long, penetrating look and said, "We would really like to know what's going on. And that rabbit looks good. Give me a piece. I love rabbit."

He reached out to the embers. He had only three fingers and a thumb.

Ima said, "It's not cooked yet."

"I don't mind," the tengu said, and crammed the half-raw rabbit's leg into his wide mouth.

"He's your brother, isn't he?" he said indistinctly.

"Who?" Mu said, thinking for a moment he meant Ima.

"So-called Master Kikuta, who claims to be Aku-zenji's son and the new King of the Mountain."

"Kiku?" Mu said, with pain, after a long pause.

"Is that his name? Kiku meaning the flower, or Kiku meaning 'listen'?"

"Listen, I think." Mu had never heard of the flower.

"Well, he writes it like the flower these days, with a fancy crest to go with it, a crest that now appears on the robes of fifty warriors and is stamped on tons of goods going between Kitakami and the east, by road and by sea."

He had said all this while chewing vigorously, blood

and grease running down his chin. Now he swallowed and reached for another piece.

"You know more than we do," Mu said. "Why have you come to ask us? We can tell you nothing you don't already know. We have not seen or heard from our brothers since they left in the ninth month. Before that, they were away for years." He pressed his lips together, trying to master the agony of remembering.

The tengu watched him intently over the rabbit bone he was chewing. He bit into it with his powerful teeth and sucked out the marrow noisily.

"And what were you doing all that time?" There was a note of accusation in his voice that Mu did not care for.

"What business is it of yours?"

The tengu hissed through his teeth in annoyance. "If I am informed correctly, you are the son of several powerful men and a sorceress of the Old People. I daresay you have many talents. Yet you are skulking here with the half-dead—and even they are ceasing to live—only kept from death yourself by the efforts of your brother, who may not have your abilities but is a lot more practical than you."

"How can you tell that?" Mu said. "You've only known us for five minutes!"

"I know many things. I am not without some supernatural ability myself," the tengu said smugly. Then he addressed Ima in a kind voice. "This rabbit is delicious. Well caught! Well cooked! In fact, well done, all around."

Ima narrowed his eyes and said nothing. Kinpoge peeked out from behind him.

"Ah, a little child!" the tengu exclaimed. "I love children!"

Not in the same way you love rabbit, I hope, Mu said to himself.

"So, what have you been doing?" the tengu repeated.

"Nothing," Mu admitted. "What should I be doing?" He recalled his nightmares and immediately wanted to defend himself. "I have no one to teach me anything. Those you say are my fathers are either dead or distant—either way, they are no use to me and never have been. So I can do certain things real, ordinary people can't, but, as you pointed out, here in the Darkwood Ima's skills are more useful. I can take on invisibility to surprise my daughter, or use the second self to make her laugh, but even that I don't do often, and when I needed to, seriously, I was too slow. I was tied up for days, and now I am half-crippled."

"Your brother tied you up?"

"Not himself, but on his orders. A warrior who serves him, called Tsunetomo."

"I know Tsunetomo. He leads the band they called the Crippled Army."

"Who are they?" Mu said. "Maybe I should join them."

"Well, it's a possibility," the tengu replied. "But that's some time ahead. They are a bunch of warriors, both Kakizuki and Miboshi, seriously injured in battle, mutilated, scarred, some blind, some without arms, some legless. They became ugly and imperfect and were turned out by their former masters, to starve to death or become bandits. Most of them are thickheads, but one or two among them have picked up some knowledge of this and that. Tsunetomo is not a complete idiot. Now they serve your brother, Master Kikuta. At first he seemed just another ambitious merchant, good at seizing opportunities and ruthless in eliminating his rivals—there are many men like that in Kitakami, but this year something changed." The tengu had been staring into the flames as he spoke. Now he fixed Mu with his glittering eyes and said, "He has acquired some magic object from which he derives extreme power."

Ima looked across at Mu and their eyes locked. Mu raised his eyebrows slightly and Ima made an almost imperceptible movement with his head. The tengu intrigued Mu, and, somewhat to his surprise, he felt he could trust him.

"It is a skull," he said slowly. "The head was taken from the monk Gessho by Shikanoko when he killed him, and after Shisoku was killed in the same fight. Shisoku was the sorcerer who lived here, and made the creatures."

"I know Shisoku," the tengu said impatiently. "Or knew, I should say."

"It was buried for years," Mu went on. "Kiku returned to retrieve it and invest it with power in secret rituals."

"Were these rituals conducted by himself alone?"

"With a woman," Mu forced himself to say. "A fox woman."

"Mu's wife," Ima explained.

Mu steeled himself to meet the tengu's eyes. He felt

they saw deep into his heart, even into his soul. They examined him without pity, saw through all the defenses he might erect, all the excuses he might make.

"Your name is Mu?" the tengu said. "Is that Mu written as 'warrior' or Mu written as 'nothing'?"

"I don't know. I have never seen it written."

"Well, when I have finished with you, you will be both. You will be a great warrior, but you will be as nothing, free from all attachments. That is what I am going to teach you."

The tengu spoke with such assurance, Mu could not help laughing. "You speak as though I have no choice in the matter."

"That is correct."

"What is your purpose?" Mu asked.

"I'm not going to tell you." The tengu cackled with sudden brusque laughter. "Not yet, anyway."

The tengu started the next day, waking Mu before it was light. There had been a deep frost in the night and the surface of the snow crackled beneath their feet when they walked outside.

"Since it is winter, we will start with a lesson on how to stay warm," the tengu announced. He surveyed Mu by the light of a flaming branch he had plucked from the fire. "Look at you! There is nothing to you. You are as frail as a dead spider. Don't you eat anything?"

"I eat plenty," Mu said, trying not to shiver.

"I saw you last night, toying with a tiny bit of rabbit, drowning your appetite with that vile twig brew. You should have grabbed that carcass and shoved the whole thing in your mouth. That's what Master Kikuta would do!"

"My daughter and my brother needed to eat, too," Mu said. He had intended his voice to be mild, but it came out whiny. "Not to mention you, Sir Tengu, our honored guest."

The tengu cackled. "Sir Tengu! That's a good one. No one's called me that before."

"Do you have a name?" Mu said.

"You can call me Tadashii, because I am always right. Now, to work. Watch this."

He handed the burning torch to Mu and began to breathe in a rapid rhythm. The snow beneath his feet melted immediately, steaming as he sank through the frozen surface down to the buried grass. Standing next to the tengu, Mu felt the heat radiate from him, making him believe for a moment that winter was over and spring had come.

"Now you do it," Tadashii said.

"Just like that? You aren't going to give me any instructions?"

"It should be second nature for you, just like the other skills that you've neglected. Imitate my breathing and think of the warmth of your own blood. That's all I'm going to tell you."

Tadashii took the smoldering branch back from Mu, waving it in the air so sparks flew from it and it crackled into flame again.

Mu began to breathe in the same rapid way as Tadashii had. He was watching the branch's fiery arc when suddenly he felt its heat inside his belly. His blood began to boil, racing through his veins. The snow steamed around him as he sank through it to the grass beneath. He felt mud under his feet.

"Ha! Ha! Ha!" Tadashii's laughter rang out through the silent forest. "Easy as breathing, isn't it?"

Mu did not reply at once. Within himself something was melting like the snow. He saw a life beyond the great drifts of grief that had all but buried him, a life where warmth and laughter—and power—were all possible again.

"What else am I going to learn?" he said.

"Everything," Tadashii promised. "I am going to teach you everything. It will be very hard work, but fun, too."

❋

It was hard work such as Mu had never known, but he reveled in it. All that he had felt was empty was now filled. He no longer dreamed of Shida or yearned after the foxlight that flickered in the marsh. He had a new purpose: to meet every challenge Tadashii threw at him and to master it. He stopped caring what the tengu's intentions might be. The training had no end other than itself. By the time summer came he could use his own innate skills flawlessly and he had learned much more: the art of sword and bow; the roots and herbs of the forest that poisoned or cured; the names and properties of trees, plants, animals, insects; how to trap a stoat, whose meat when dried was a source of courage; how to track bears and wolves; how to recognize scorpions, spiders, snakes, and toads, and milk their venom.

His physical strength increased, as Tadashii showed him how to use his muscles and how to build them up. For hours he carried boulders the length of the stream and back again, and while he would never approach the tengu in strength—Tadashii could lift great rocks with one hand—he surpassed most ordinary men, despite his slight build and appearance. He was no longer lame. He kept the stick, but as a weapon. Tadashii forged a sword for him.

Tadashii could not give Mu wings, but he showed him how to leap to great heights, how to swing from treetop to treetop like a monkey, how to stride the crags like a mountain goat. He seemed to have an inexhaustible patience, which he also taught to Mu. Indeed, Mu thought he must have a different sense of time for, though he had spoken with some urgency on their first meeting, now he seemed to be in no hurry, either to solve the problem of Master Kikuta or to leave.

The seasons passed. It was winter again, and then another winter. Often in the long dark nights they played Go or checkers or chess, for the tengu loved all games, but still he gave no indication of what his original purpose might have been.

❊

One spring night, two years after the tengu arrived, he took Mu by the shoulders and flew with him high above the forest toward the side of the mountain. It was the night of the full moon of the third month and they could see as clearly as if it were day. Mu caught a glimpse of water that was Lake Kasumi, and the river that flowed from it all the way to the capital, and, in the other direction, the Northern Sea.

Tadashii landed on a ledge where rocks had been placed in a circle, dropping Mu gently in the center of them. On each rock perched winged tengu; some, like Tadashii, had beaks, others long red noses. They were all armed with swords and bows. To see so many at once was alarming. Mu had landed on his hands and knees and he now turned this into a deep, reverent bow.

"Welcome," said a number of voices, all low and gruff, like Tadashii's.

"So this is your pupil?" said one long-nosed being.

"It is," Tadashii replied. "His name is Mu, the warrior of nothingness."

"Does he understand the principles of being and non-being, of form and no-form?" the tengu asked.

"That's not as important as being able to play a good game," another tengu interrupted. "Is he going to be a player or a stone on the board?"

"That is not yet decided," Tadashii said. "I am hoping you, my masters, will look on him favorably and instruct him."

"If he is able to learn we will teach him. Let us see if he can survive our lessons." There was a ripple of laughter, as if the tengu did not really believe that was possible.

Tadashii touched Mu's head. "Be strong," he whispered. "I hope we meet again."

Mu shivered slightly. The uncharacteristic affection alarmed him as much as Tadashii's words. There was a faint rush of air against his face, as Tadashii flexed his wings, followed by a greater rush as all the tengu rose into the air, leaving him alone on the mountainside.

Alone, but not alone. Physically the tengu might have departed, but they were still present in some way, observing Mu, as the moon set and the stars wheeled overhead. He settled, cross-legged, in the meditation position Tadashii had taught him, reminding himself he had been tied up for a week, in a far more uncomfortable way, and had survived. The first light of dawn filled the sky and birds began to sing piercingly. The mountain air was cold, heavy with dew. Mu warmed himself, almost without thinking. The hours passed. He was neither hungry nor thirsty. He had no needs and no desires. He knew only the eternal being that includes all life, all death, in which each person exists for a tiny moment and is then absorbed back into the endless void of all and nothing.

He knew he had great powers; he saw they were meaningless. He embraced the nothingness of his name.

He lost all track of time. He seemed to take leave of his body and fly above the land. At first it looked like a Go board and then more like a vast scroll, presenting various scenes to him. He left the Darkwood behind and soared over Lake Kasumi. He saw the lake was shrinking, its marshlands drying out, a rim of half-dried, foul-smelling mud clogging its beaches. He was above a city, to the north of the lake. Could this be Kitakami? He peered down, through buildings that seemed to have no roofs, so he could see straight into them. He saw Kiku, grown older, surrounded by servants and retainers. Mu perceived the network of his business empire, spreading like a spider's web over the land.

Then the wind took him and blew him to the south. He saw a young woman on a pleasure boat, entertaining a man who looked like a merchant, one of Kiku's rivals perhaps, and he looked deep down into the lake, where someone lay hidden, breathing through a reed. To his surprise, he recognized Chika. On the shore red lanterns denoted a festival. A troupe of acrobats were performing with monkeys. Mu noticed a strong, well-built boy, about twelve or thirteen years old, and an older lad, maybe in his twenties, wiry and flexible, a natural performer, with attractive, expressive features, who kept the crowd spellbound. A young girl of the same age beat time on a drum, her eyes fixed on the performer. A large black bird with a sprinkle of gold feathers hovered above him and it suddenly soared upward, as if it sensed Mu's presence. He saw its bright yellow eyes searching, but it did not see him.

Now he was over the capital, floating above mansions and palaces. In a sumptuous room a great lord, his face gray-tinged and gaunt, was retching into a silver bowl. Outside, warriors and noblemen gathered anxiously. Along the riverbank were strewn corpses. Dogs scavenged among them. The river was a thin, dirty trickle. He was above a temple, newly built from gleaming cypress and cedar. Again he could see straight down into the halls and cloisters. An old man sat with a lute on his knees. He seemed to be dozing, but as Mu passed overhead he startled and turned his face upward, listening. Mu saw into the depths of the lake, where a sleeping dragon lay coiled, its scales shimmering dully in the murky water. A swirling motion began, a whirlpool formed, the dragon stretched and flexed. In the main hall of the temple a figure knelt, chanting sutras, before an altar where golden statues and painted deities kept watch. A woman's voice rose and circled around the lutist's song. The notes vibrated and echoed against one another until the friction became unbearable. At the edges of the land, smoke was rising, as when a scroll is first thrown on the fire. Its edges blacken, it begins to contort in the heat, scorch marks appear here and there, finally flames seize hold.

The land is about to burn, Mu realized.

Only the Darkwood seemed untouched. With a sense of gratitude and relief, he turned back to its dark green mass. He and Tadashii had made many journeys through the forest, but now Mu went farther than he ever had before. He was shown a building hidden among the trees, high in the mountains, a small shrine perhaps, or a hermit's retreat. Looking down through the canopy of leaves he saw two silver-gray horses grazing in a clearing. Nearby a wolflike creature kept watch.

Gen!

In the clearing were four figures involved in an intricate dance. One was clearly a woman, though she dressed like a man. Two wore black cloths over their faces, covering everything but their eyes. The fourth wore a mask, a stag's head with one broken antler.

"Shikanoko!" Mu cried.

Shikanoko looked up, the only person to notice Mu's presence. Unlike the bird, he could see him. Mu felt their eyes meet and lock, but before he could speak he sensed he was losing the power of flight. For a moment he thought he would plummet to earth, and he almost blacked out as he rushed through the air, but he calmed himself and summoned his concentration, and found himself with a thump back on his mountain ledge.

Tadashii was sitting waiting for him. "Not a very elegant landing," he said. "But otherwise, my masters have reported you did quite well. You have seen the state of the board. I hope we will soon be ready for my next move."

"Do you think you could explain a little more clearly?" Mu said.

The tengu did not reply.

"I saw many strange things that I don't understand," Mu persisted.

"Meditate on them." Tadashii refused to say anything else.

❋

Her father was so preoccupied during the years of the tengu's training, he hardly noticed Kinpoge growing up. She turned more and more to Ima, who took care of her, fed her, and taught her how to hunt and to cook. She liked to catch fish, taking them out of the water with her bare hands; she knew where to gather fern heads and burdock, mushrooms and chestnuts. She looked after the fake animals that remained and, particularly, the skull horse, Ban. She gave it grass and water every morning and, in the evenings, rode it through the air. She wove reins for Ban from the green rushes, and tied two cross pieces onto the pole, one as a handhold and one for her feet. In spring and summer she made garlands of flowers and decorated the skull.

Sometimes she wished she had a real horse, but, as Ima pointed out, a real horse could not fly and it would grow old and die, whereas Kiku had, unwittingly, given Ban another kind of life.

Ban responded to her attentions, turned its head to her when she approached, and leaped joyfully into the air when she untethered it.

She did not go far from the hut where she had lived all her life. Mountains surrounded it and she did not think Ban could fly that high. But she often followed the course of the stream that flowed past the hut. After a few miles, it divided into two, one branch continuing to the west, the other turning southward. Once she had gone south, but after a while the land became cultivated and there were too many people around. She knew instinctively that she should keep hidden and that she should never give away the location of the hut.

So, instead, she and Ban explored the west branch, which flowed through a steep, thickly wooded valley. Occasionally she saw movements in the trees and she realized monkeys lived there.

The monkeys fascinated her. She watched the mothers and babies with a kind of hunger—she who had hardly known her own mother. The mothers took such good care of the babies. In the summer they roamed carefree through the forest, leaping from tree to tree like her father, and in winter they gathered around the pools of the hot springs. Kinpoge spied on them through the branches of the leafless trees. Once or twice they noticed the skull horse and shrieked in alarm, as they did when eagles flew overhead.

One day, near sunset, it was maybe her tenth or eleventh spring on earth—like her father she had matured quickly and was nearly an adult—she and Ban were hovering over the thick canopy, hoping to catch sight of the monkeys, when a boy's face popped out through the leaves, staring at her in astonishment. She could not tell his age, but he seemed taller than she was. His eyes were long and narrow, his nose rather sharp, his cheekbones high. The sun's rays shone round him like a halo.

"Hello!" he exclaimed, and then, hurriedly, "Don't be frightened! Don't leave!"

Ban was quivering beneath Kinpoge's hands. She knew she should escape quickly, but then the boy pulled himself a little higher so his feet were planted firmly in the crook of the branches, and stood up. Two monkeys pushed through the leaves. One climbed onto his shoulders, peering at Kinpoge and Ban and chattering excitedly. The other sat beside the boy, holding on to his leg with one hand and scratching his own belly with the other.

"Who are you?" the boy said. "Are you some magic creature? You must be, for you are so small and you are riding a very strange-looking steed. Do you understand human speech?" When she did not reply he persisted. "Do you speak some fairy language?" He began to mime his words with extravagant gestures that made her laugh.

"I understand you," she called across the space between them.

"What's your name? Mine is Takemaru—everyone calls me Take—but that's a child's name. Soon I will take an adult name, for I am nearly grown up."

"Kinpoge," she said.

"Like the flower? That is so beautiful. And it suits you, you are so small and bright! Where do you live? In the treetops?"

"I live with my father and my uncle. A little way upstream. I must go now."

"Come again," he said. "I will look out for you."

"Goodbye!" Kinpoge cried, turning Ban's head to the east.

She did not tell her father or Ima about the encounter. Both had warned her never to let herself be seen, never to talk to anyone. But she could not stop thinking about the boy, Takemaru, and she wanted very much to see him again. The next day she wove a fresh garland of spring flowers for Ban and, in the afternoon, she set out again. She knew she should not fly toward the west, but somehow she could not help it.

The days were lengthening and there were still

several hours before nightfall. The sun in the west daz-
zled her. It made the shiny new green leaves glisten as
they danced in the breeze. It was the fourth month and
already very hot. There was no sign of rain and even the
dew, which usually soaked the forest every night, had
dried up. Every tree was familiar to her and she could
tell each one was suffering. They had responded to the
demands of the season and had put out new leaves, but
it had cost them; they were becoming frail, their roots
no longer held firmly by the embracing earth.

She guided Ban to the same tree and there was the
boy, alone this time. His face lit up when he saw her and
he held out his hand. Kinpoge took it and, still holding
Ban's bridle so the skull horse could not fly away, stepped
nimbly onto the branch.

The tree swayed in the wind, the leaves rustled, the
humming of insects rose around them. There was a
strong, heady smell of blossoms and catkins. Take held
her firmly.

"I'm all right," she said, easing herself from his
grasp and sitting down astride the branch. "I won't
fall."

"You should be an acrobat," he said, sitting down
facing her. "You are so light and adroit. But, I don't know
why, girls never are, only boys. Even Kai, who is agile
like you, has to be content with playing the drum."

"I don't know what you're talking about," she said.
They were so close, their knees almost touched. "What's
an acrobat? Is it something to do with the monkeys?"

"In a way. We do tricks with the monkeys. People

like to watch us. They give us food, clothes, even coins sometimes. We go to all the markets and every year, at this time, we come to the forest to look for suitable monkeys to train—do you know what train means?"

"I do!" Kinpoge screwed up her face. "My father is being trained by a tengu. It's been going on for years. I hope your monkeys don't take as long!"

"A tengu?" She could tell this interested Take very much. "A real tengu? What is he teaching him?"

"Everything. But mostly how to fight with sword and bow."

"How to kill people?" Take's eyes gleamed.

"I suppose so, though I think it's more about not letting them kill you, as far as I can see. And then there's a lot of meditation and spiritual exercises. My father is often absent for weeks and when he comes back he seems like a different person."

"Different in what way?" Take asked, and then added quietly, "I have never known my father."

"You haven't missed much. Fathers are very tiresome, at least mine is. He has seen and learned things most people don't know about. Well, I can't really say what most people do or don't know, as you are the only real person I've met. But the tengu teaches him secrets and shows him hidden things."

Take sighed. "I'd give anything for that kind of instruction. I feel I should have been born to the way of the sword and the bow. But the acrobats I grew up among follow a different path. They will not kill anything. They eat only fruit and plants."

"Come back with me," Kinpoge said eagerly. "Ima, my uncle, will make you roast hare or a meat stew. And we'll ask my father if he will share the tengu's teaching with you."

❋

Ima was out in the forest, somewhere. Mu was alone, going through the rigorous exercises he followed every day. The tengu no longer lived at the hut—he had gone away on a mission he did not reveal—but Mu continued to work as if Tadashii still breathed down his neck with his hot peppery breath and clacked his beak in admonishment.

He was inside the hut, in front of the altar that Shisoku had made years before. The tengu had shown him the meaning of all the objects the old hermit had collected: the augury sticks, the reed arrows, the protective carvings made of peachwood, the panels depicting the twelve cardinal points, the twelve-month guardians, the twelve animals of the cycle of the years. He had explained how to use them, and access their power, just as he had explained the curses that lay sealed, with the five poisonous creatures, in their jars—curses that killed an enemy and then controlled his soul.

Mu had grown up among these things and had never appreciated their power, though Kiku had. His brother had known enough to perform rituals in this place, with the fox woman, Shida. After that time, Mu could hardly bear to enter the hut and at one time had wanted to burn it down. Through Tadashii's teaching, he had faced that pain and humiliation and seen them as illusions of heart and mind. The memory no longer touched him.

He did not like to be interrupted or even watched. Usually, Kinpoge and Ima kept out of his way. But now his daughter's voice broke into the clear well his mind had become, sending unwelcome ripples through it. At first he ignored her, wanting to stay in that removed state of concentration that had become the source of knowledge and power for him, but her voice was as sharp and insistent as a crow's.

"Father! Father, where are you? I've brought someone to meet you."

He heard steps right outside and leaped to his feet. He did not want to let any stranger in. Taking on invisibility, he slipped through the doorway. For a moment, unseen, he studied them: the girl, his child, her ragged clothes and unkempt hair, her small face appearing like the pale moon among dark clouds, her bare arms and legs, scratched and scarred. And alongside her the boy, tall, handsome, he supposed, with the face of a young warrior, but wearing strange red clothes, his hair tied in a topknot, his shoulders unexpectedly broad for his age, his arms and legs as muscled as a grown man's. He recognized him, and after a moment remembered he had seen him on his flight over the land. What did that mean? That he and the other acrobat and the girl drummer were all somehow connected to him and Tadashii? Despite this, the sight of him filled Mu with a kind of unreasoning anger. It would be a pleasure to kill him.

He was surprised by the anger. It was a long time since his peace of mind had been disturbed by emotion. He looked at it dispassionately and let it slip away.

Then he said quietly, "Kinpoge. I am here." He let himself be seen.

They both turned at the sound of his voice, the boy with a startled expression on his face, the girl more exasperated.

"Don't play tricks on us, Father!"

"Surely we walked right past . . . how did we not see him?" the boy whispered in Kinpoge's ear. Mu heard him clearly.

"It's just something he does. I told you he was tiresome." Kinpoge held the skull horse by the woven reins. She gave it a perfunctory pat and thrust its pole into the ground.

"Did the tengu teach him?"

"He's always been able to do it. But he's got better at it, since the tengu came."

It amused Mu to hear Kinpoge's assessment of his progress. He was smiling, as the boy approached him, which must have encouraged him, for he bowed his head and said boldly, "Sir, my name is Takemaru. There's no reason why you should show me any favor, but your daughter has told me about your great skill and, well . . ." His formal tone deserted him and he dropped to his knees. "I have no one to teach me how to fight with the sword and the bow. Please let me become your pupil."

"What a ridiculous idea," Mu said, neither moving

nor bowing. "Go away. Don't come back. Kinpoge, you are not to meet him again."

As the boy raised his head Mu saw the disappointment in his face. Kinpoge said, "Father, please!"

"Don't argue! It's impossible. Now go away." Mu settled himself, cross-legged, and pretended to tend the fire.

"I'd better go," Takemaru said.

"I'll come and see you again." Kinpoge's voice was thin with emotion.

"No, if your father forbids it, you must not," he said seriously. "You must obey your father."

"Quite right," Mu remarked. "Now get going!"

"Goodbye, sir. Goodbye, Lady Kinpoge." He bowed formally and began to walk away, his back straight, his stride proud.

"Wait!" Kinpoge cried. "I'll go with you. I'll show you the way."

"Stay here," Mu ordered.

He sensed the conflict within her between desire and obedience. He saw her struggle and then, suddenly, with no warning, the second self emerged. He had seen it so often in his brothers and, since the tengu's arrival, he had used it himself, with increasingly refined mastery, but he had not really expected his daughter to have the same skills. The shadow Kinpoge began to flit after the boy who walked resolutely on, ignorant of what was happening behind him. The real Kinpoge wavered for a moment. Her eyes began to roll backward. Mu caught her as she fell.

The other Kinpoge faded as the two selves merged. He splashed water on her face and rubbed her wrists. After a moment she opened her eyes.

"What happened?"

"You did one of my tiresome tricks," Mu said.

"Was I invisible?"

"No, there were two of you. You discovered your second self."

"Really? It felt strange."

"You will learn to control it," he said, "and use it when you want to."

"How exciting!" Kinpoge's eyes gleamed. "But I'd really like to be able to become invisible."

"Maybe that will come, too." It made Mu sad. She was almost grown up. What would become of her? Who would marry her? Who would look after her when he and Ima passed on? The tengu had promised he would be free of all attachments, but this one for his daughter obstinately remained.

She lay in his arms, in a way she had not since she was a child. They were still sitting like that when Ima returned carrying a large dead hare. He looked at them but said nothing, then began to build up the fire, which had almost burned out, with exaggerated care.

"Uncle, I used the second self," Kinpoge announced.

"You did? I thought you would sooner or later!"

"You expected it?" Mu said. "I didn't. It took me by surprise."

"You only have to consider who her father is, and her mother, for that matter," Ima replied.

While the fire burned brightly, producing the glow-ing embers that would roast the hare, Ima skinned the creature and removed the entrails. Kinpoge took the skin down to the creek. Two of the dogs followed her hopefully. Mu could hear the scrape of the knife on the skin. The fur was thick and soft. They sewed the hides together to make blankets for winter.

The meat smelled fragrant as it began to roast. He thought it would bring her back soon; she was always hungry. Then his sharp ears caught another voice. The dogs barked and fled back to the fire.

"Hello, little girl. That smells good. I think I will stay for supper." The tengu stepped out of the shadows and jumped nimbly across the stream.

Kinpoge dropped the skin and the knife, and hugged him. Tadashii picked her up with one hand, set her on his shoulders, and walked toward the fire.

"It's not cooked yet," Ima warned before he could say anything. "Don't touch it!"

"You know I don't mind raw meat," Tadashii replied sulkily.

Kinpoge slipped down to the ground. "Let's play a game while we wait."

"Maybe later," he said. "I need to talk to your father."

"Did you finish cleaning the skin?" Ima said to Kinpoge.

"Nearly," she replied.

"Well, go and finish it. Then string it up where the animals can't reach it." Ima's voice, as always, was kindly but firm. Kinpoge usually obeyed him, without question, whereas she tested her father, arguing with him endlessly. Now she went back to the bank of the stream and picked up the hare skin. From the way she shook it, Mu guessed it was already crawling with ants.

"Let's go inside," the tengu suggested.

Mu looked at Ima before he agreed, but his brother was staring at the hare as it sizzled in the embers, and did not return his gaze.

When they were in the hut, the tengu bowed respectfully in the direction of the altar and sat cross-legged on the floor. Mu sat opposite him, just where he had been a short time ago when Kinpoge had called him.

"Don't feel sorry for him," the tengu said.

"Who?" Mu's thoughts had progressed to the boy, Takemaru.

"Your brother, Ima."

Mu shrugged. "I don't, on the whole. But sometimes it seems a little unfair. We were all born at the same time from the same mother. None of us chose our parents or our circumstances. Yet Kiku, Kuro, and I have talents our brothers don't have."

"Fair, unfair, these words have no meaning for me." Tadashii dismissed the idea with a contemptuous wave of his four-fingered hand. "Your brother Ku is perfectly happy being a servant to Master Kikuta in Kitakami. And Ima has talents you still don't appreciate. He plays a very good game of chess, for example. He is content with his life, isn't he?"

"I don't know. Is he?"

The tengu scowled, as though he was unable to

answer this. "That's not what I've come to talk to you about," he said.

Mu raised his eyebrows and remained silent.

"I sent you a pupil," said the tengu. "And you sent him away."

"You sent him?"

"Well, not in so many words. But I intended him to come."

"You could have told me," Mu replied.

"I expect you to discern this sort of thing," Tadashii said, sounding irritated. "Didn't you recognize him and guess who he might be?"

"He told me his name was Takemaru."

"Takeyoshi is his real name. He is the son of Shika-noko and the Autumn Princess. He has come to the Darkwood with the one they call Yoshi, Yoshimori, the true emperor. Neither of them know who they are. They think they are monkey boys and acrobats. We need you to teach Takeyoshi to be a warrior, join forces with your brother, find Shikanoko, and offer him these forces so the Emperor might be restored and Heaven placated. Then we can get back to normal."

Mu recalled the acrobats he had seen, the girl with the drum. "Is that what it's all been for?" he said. He gazed past the tengu's face at the objects of power clustered all around him, some on shelves, hidden in awe of their effect, beneath seven-layered cloths or in boxes within boxes.

"Well, it's part of a plan we came up with. Out of desperation, if you must know."

"Why don't you teach him?" Mu asked.

"I might, in due course. In fact, I must. An injustice was done a long time ago that I am trying to put right. Something that was stolen must be recovered. But it is hard for me to make contact with a fully human person who has no knowledge of the other worlds. You have shown that you can travel between them. You will be my bridge to Takeyoshi. It's your turn to be the teacher. You never know how complete your learning is until you pass it on. You could call it the ultimate stage. And the other parts of your mission could not be achieved by anyone else. You alone can be reconciled with your brother. You alone can find Shikanoko."

"I saw him," Mu said. "That time I flew. He is in the Darkwood, but far to the north."

"Very good!" Tadashii seemed more pleased than Mu had ever known him before, and even though he suspected the tengu was flattering him so Mu would carry out his wishes, he still felt a warm glow from the praise.

"I thought I saw a woman there with him," he said, "and two men."

"We hope the woman is going to kill the man called Masachika," the tengu said. "And the men are known as the Burnt Twins. Shikanoko has to be brought back to this world. If he stays much longer in the Dark-wood he will become a deerlike creature, and if he dies his spirit will be that of a stag, possibly a god, but he will not be able either to enter the pure land or to be reborn."

"When I saw him he wore the deer mask and was dancing," Mu said.

"He is close to the edge. Soon he will be beyond saving. Unless the mask is removed by a pure spirit who loves him, he will be lost."

"Is there any such person?" Mu remembered the raw emotion with which Kiku had revealed what happened at Ryusonji. "He loved the Autumn Princess, but she is dead."

"I don't know much about that side of human life," Tadashii said. "I've observed there are certain acts that bring pleasure and produce children—that's all very well, I suppose, but why complicate it?"

Mu said, "There is passion, and jealousy, the desire to possess another, the fear of losing her."

"But you have put all that behind you, haven't you?"

"I suppose so," Mu said. "Living here, I haven't had much choice."

"I'm glad, though, that you seem to know something about it, for you may recognize such a person."

"It could be any one of us," Mu said. "We all loved and respected Shikanoko."

"I think it has to be female," Tadashii said bluntly.

"What about the woman I saw?"

The tengu laughed, in a coarse way. "No, she is not for him."

"Which should I do first?" Mu asked, thinking about the various tasks that lay ahead of him.

"Follow your nose," Tadashii said, tapping his own beak and cackling.

"Should I go after this Takeyoshi and bring him back?" Mu said.

"You have missed the opportunity," the tengu replied. "It will be another year before he returns to the Darkwood. Next time, don't turn him away."

9

YOSHI

That was one of the best performances we've ever done, Yoshi thought as he walked toward where Kai sat with her drum balanced between her knees. It was a warm, still night—too hot for early spring—but the drought seemed more bearable once darkness came and the brilliant stars appeared in the clear sky. Crowds lately had been harder to please. People had more serious concerns: their crops, their children's health, shortages of food, ever-increasing taxes. It had been a hard winter followed as usual by the most difficult time of year. Spring brought more work but less food and in the warmer weather diseases spread more rapidly. Tonight at the start the crowd had been sullen, even hostile, but by the end they were laughing.

I won them over! he thought with pride, for he knew it was he they stayed to watch. The music and the monkeys caught their attention, but it was his performance that kept them spellbound. Saru had always been popular and had taught Yoshi everything he knew, but now Yoshi's leaps, somersaults, and back flips had more daring and assurance, looked more dangerous, yet never failed. The monkeys were inspired by him, would do anything he asked of them, and watched him with devoted eyes.

He was not sure of his exact age but knew he was at the height of his ability. He had seen the older men age suddenly before they were thirty. Their life was physically hard and the demands they made on their bodies huge. He himself probably did not have many years left, but at the moment he was the shining star, the sun, the moon, of the troupe.

Saru called, "We're going back to the boat to eat."

The villagers had been generous in the end, but they had little to share: a basket with four eggs, a handful of early greens, little cakes of millet and dried seaweed. The acrobats were always hungry. Performing and traveling used up so much energy, and none of them ate meat or fish, having taken vows since childhood to take no life, not animal or insect, and certainly not human.

Yoshi made a gesture to show he'd heard him. No doubt Saru would be annoyed, but Yoshi was going to speak to Kai and make sure she came with them. Nothing else made Saru jealous, but this would. Yoshi knew Saru loved him as much as the monkeys did. They had grown up together and shared everything in life. But Kai had known Yoshi in his other life, which no one else knew about, and which he never talked about. She was as close to him and as essential as one of his own limbs.

He studied her as he went toward her. The torchlight fell on her face, which was flushed with the thrill of performing, and reflected in her shining eyes. A piece of material wound around her head held her hair back and hid her ears, but she pulled it away as he approached and let her hair fall around her. He was still half-drunk with the applause and the excitement and a wave of desire for her swept over him.

Lady Fuji had tried to keep Kai away from the acrobats, telling her she must stay with the family of musicians who had adopted her, but no one could stop Kai doing what she wanted, especially once she turned sixteen and came of age. She scorned any suggestion that she might marry one of the boys she had grown up with, and while she still played on the pleasure boats with the musicians, she joined the acrobats whenever she could and beat her drum for them. She had no fear of water, and she followed them around the lake in her own boat. A fisherman from Aomizu had vanished from this vessel one night. The next day it could be seen bobbing about on the waves. Sometimes it seemed there was a figure in it; sometimes it looked empty. No one dared go near it in case it had become possessed by the spirit who had pulled the unfortunate man into the water and who might drown them, too. But Kai swam out to it and brought it back to shore, had it blessed by the old priest with whom the acrobats worshipped, and from then on navigated it skillfully from shore to shore, followed by flocks of blue-and-white herons with whom she seemed to have a deep connection, calling to them and imitating their harsh cries. Often Yoshi would find himself thinking of her and would soon after hear the splash of the single oar and see her shape outlined against the evening sky and feel his heart expand with sheer joy.

About a year before, on another spring evening, they had become lovers. He had seen her out on the lake and had waited for her after the others had packed up and left to find shelter for the night. She had jumped out of the boat straight into his arms as though the moment had been preordained by the gods. He had pushed her hair back and kissed her tiny, unformed ears. The boat had drifted off into deep water and Kai had broken away from him to swim after it and pull it back to shore. They were both laughing with happiness as she took off her wet clothes and he pulled her close to warm her, feeling all the curves and planes of her body and marveling at how he fitted perfectly against them, then within them.

Now he held her again, remembering that time, re-capturing its thrill and ecstasy. She was trembling and her eyes were full of longing as she led him to a deserted part of the beach and they lay down together under the stars.

Afterward as he rested, spent, against her, caressing her silky skin, there was a sharp call and he heard the beat of wings as Kon settled on a rock nearby.

"He never leaves you," Kai said. "I would worry more about you if Kon were not always watching over you."

"He doesn't actually do anything," Yoshi replied, "except irritate me. He hides for a while among other birds, and I think he's gone, but he always reappears again."

"Kon bears witness to who you are," Kai said quietly. "I think I would have forgotten if it weren't for him."

"Better if we all forget it." Yoshi eased himself away from her a little.

"How much do you remember?" They had never spoken about their past, their childhood in the palace, their flight from the burning city. "Do you remember the day the werehawk came? It was after that that everything began to change. It knew you, then. It bowed to you. Was that Kon, or another one?"

"Let's not talk about it," Yoshi muttered.

"We need to." She took his hand and laid it on her belly. "Your child is growing inside me. Can you feel how my body is changing?" She guided his hand to her breasts. "See how they are heavier and fuller. It will be born in the winter of this year."

He wanted to make love to her again, but she hesitated. "If you are the true emperor," she whispered in a tiny voice, "you cannot be kept from the Lotus Throne. Who are we to try to defy the will of Heaven? But then we will be separated. What will become of our child?"

"I am just Yoshimaru, the monkey boy," he whispered back. "We have kept it secret for so long, we will continue to do so. We will be a family. You are my wife. It's what I've always wanted ever since we were children. You must know that."

"I do," she replied. "I remember being told all the time that I would never be suitable for you because of my ears, and I used to cry myself to sleep at the thought of you marrying someone else."

"We had the luck to end up together in a world where these things don't matter," Yoshi said. "If your ears were not misshapen, Fuji would have taken you for her own trade." He kissed first one, then the other. "We should be thankful to them."

"It's only that when Akihime saved your life and we fled from the palace, you said, 'If I am to reign I cannot die now.' Do you remember that?"

"I was just a child," Yoshi said. "I didn't understand anything. After Saru and the others found me in the forest, for a long time I expected Akihime to come back for me. I dreaded it. When I heard she was dead I grieved for her, but then I realized she had died without giving me away, and I was profoundly grateful, but most of all relieved. I've never wanted to be anything else but an acrobat, to be with you, to follow the teachings of the Secret One, and now to have our child. If anyone finds out about me I'll be put to death. The Miboshi have their own emperor, my uncle Daigen. My death would legitimize him."

Kai pulled him close. "Then we will never breathe a word, and we will pray that Heaven continues to ignore us. No one else knows, do they?"

He did not answer her, but he was thinking of the girl pulled from the lake, the girl who had the lute, Genzo, who was now one of Lady Fuji's most popular pleasure women. She had never spoken of his secret to him and she had kept the lute hidden away. But she had known who he was in that moment on the boat, for Genzo had told her. And then there was Shikanoko. Yoshi did not know if he was alive or dead, and had never mentioned him to Kai. But he still relived that moment on the edge of the stream when he had thought he would die, and Shikanoko still strode through his dreams with his antlered mask and drawn sword.

10

HINA (YAYOI)

Lake Kasumi was drying up. Villages that had been on the water's edge were now half a mile away, and often boats ran aground as the channels became shallow. This was not the only way life had become harder for the riverbank people. For years they had escaped scrutiny, living and working as they did between the worlds, on thresholds, in the spaces between high and low water, which are neither inside nor outside, neither land nor sea. They considered themselves different from ordinary people and therefore not subject to the same laws. Everything they did had a kind of magic to it: they created wares that had not existed before and transformed them into other things by way of exchange and barter, increasingly for coins, which were themselves a numinous creation. They trained animals for entertainment and lived alongside them. They controlled and dispensed the ephemeral ecstasies of music and sex, both inexhaustible, given away freely and constantly renewed, never drying up.

These gifts were not paid for, as such, but were reciprocated with other gifts, silken robes, bolts of cloth, the finest teas and wines, ceramic bowls, carvings, parasols, prayer beads. Eventually, this came to the attention of Lord Aritomo, who could not rest unless every part of his realm was brought under his control. He made a law that all entertainers and traders should be licensed. His own officials would issue permits, in return for a share in the gifts, which suddenly turned, in a quite unmagical way, into taxable produce, providing income for Aritomo's armies, his roads, and his fortifications.

Because Yayoi could not only read and write but also calculate, and because her charm was famous, it fell to her to deal with these officials. Lady Fuji, who had built up a floating empire of pleasure boats, and who was most reluctant to share the results of her good fortune and business skills with anyone, relied on her more and more.

"I wish I could come upon some scheme to stop them bothering us," she said after one difficult encounter, when they had finally managed to make an official forget why he had paid them a visit. "I don't know what I would do without you. Truly, it must have been Heaven that sent you. Wasn't it a miracle how the wind drove the acrobats' boat across the lake to gather you up, you and Takemaru, and then changed to bring you to me?"

They had often talked about that day, twelve or more

years earlier, when Yayoi had fled from Nishimi, a baby in her arms, along with the lute and the Kudzu Vine Treasure Store. It was almost like a ritual or a ballad. Yayoi gave the expected response, hardly needing to take her attention away from her calculations, thinking fleetingly of the child she had been, when her name had been Hina.

"You and the gods saved my life that day."

"It was surely our fate, for now you are as close to me as the daughter I never had."

"I will always look after you, as if you were my own mother," Yayoi replied.

"You were not the only young girl I rescued," Fuji mused.

"I know, you have helped many who would otherwise have died."

The girls Yayoi had known at the convent had grown up like her to become the women on the pleasure boats: Asagao, still her dearest friend, Yuri, Sada, Sen, and Teru, and all the others selling their songs and smiles.

"One came like you, with a boy and a younger girl."

Yayoi marked her place with her finger and began to pay attention. Fuji was a woman of many secrets and divulged them only when it served her purpose.

"She said he was her brother. He was about six or seven, a proper little princeling. I remember explaining the sacred and the profane to him. He was afraid of pollution. And now look at him—he has lived with the monkeys for so many years, he has almost become one of them. And the little girl is Kai, the drummer."

"Which boy is that?" Yayoi said striving for calm. "I can hardly tell them apart."

"Yoshimaru. His older sister carried a lute just like yours, though she did not have your talent. I don't believe she could really play at all, yet the lute played itself, the sweetest music you've ever heard. I suppose it was enchanted in some way. Which reminds me, I haven't seen your lute for years. Do you keep it hidden away?"

Yayoi said nothing until Fuji had fallen silent for so long it seemed unnatural not to respond. "What happened to her?" Yayoi asked, though she knew better than Fuji.

"Kai was too ill to travel when the other two left us to go to Rinrakuji. We heard the temple burned down around the same time. Yoshimaru turned up with Sarumaru, and the monkeys, a few months later, but there was no sign of his sister and he's never mentioned her. I often wondered what became of her. She was not as beautiful as you, but she had a sort of wild charm, like a young boy. Her father had laid a condition of purity on her, which I would have respected. It suited her. She was to be a shrine maiden."

Neither of them spoke for a few moments. Yayoi looked out across the lake. The mountain ranges beyond were beginning to turn hazy and mauve as the sun passed over them toward the west. It would have been a perfect spring afternoon were it not for the turbid water and the exposed stretches of mud.

Fuji said, "A few months later I heard of a young girl who rode a white stallion on the roads around the lake, fighting off men, with a sword that had itself become famous. I thought it might be her, but then no more was heard of her. I suppose she is dead now. Like the Autumn Princess."

Yayoi said nothing.

"I have been thinking about her a lot, lately," Fuji said, leaning closer and dropping her voice. "Yoshimaru has become such a fine young man. And you see, dear Yayoi, if he is who I think he is, some very important people might be interested—interested enough to stop persecuting us with their demands for licenses and fees. I see you are astonished. You would never have guessed, would you, that Yoshimaru, our monkey boy, who is rather fond of the little drummer, is the missing emperor?"

"It cannot be true," Yayoi said, though she knew it was, had known ever since the lute, Genzo, had burst into melody in his presence when she had escaped from Nishimi. The ancient lute knew the true emperor. For years she had said nothing, had simply prayed for his safety, as she watched him grow from a child of eight to a young man of about twenty.

Like all the acrobats, he dressed and wore his hair in the style of childhood and still carried his childish name. He and Saru were inseparable, both handsome, lively young men. Take, the baby she had brought from Nishimi, adored them both, having been brought up by them, among the monkeys. And lately she along with everyone else had noticed that Yoshi and Kai were in love.

"Does he know?" she wondered aloud.

Fuji said, "He has never given the slightest sign. He must have forgotten. He was only six years old when we first saw him."

"We should leave things as they are," Yayoi said. "He will have a far happier life here."

"But if he is restored to the throne, maybe the drought will stop and the lake will go back to how it used to be. And we would gain considerable rewards."

"Restored to the throne? You are dreaming if you think that will happen! The Miboshi will put him to death, and probably everyone who knows of his existence!"

"You are always so pessimistic, Yayoi! You always expect the worst!" Fuji turned away, biting a hangnail in exasperation.

Isn't that how my life has turned out? Yayoi thought. *My mother passed away when I was a child, my father died at the side of the Crown Prince in the Ninpei rebellion, my little brother was killed by mistake after he had been kidnapped. My own life has been spared only through Fuji's discretion.*

Fuji spat out the nail and said in a malicious voice, "It happened when you were away at the temple so I don't believe you ever heard of it, but Lord Aritomo forced his favorite, Yukikuni no Takaakira, to commit suicide."

"I did not know," Yayoi said. "But what has it to do with me?"

"He was accused of harboring a Kakizuki girl, Kiyoyori's daughter in fact, first in Miyako and then at Nishimi." She looked up at Yayoi, her usual charming smile on her face. "Aritomo saw it as unpardonable treachery. Takaakira ripped his belly. They say it took him hours to die. Nobody knows Kiyoyori's daughter survived, except me. And you, of course."

Yayoi had not known he was dead, the man who had saved her life when the capital fell to the Miboshi. He had, undoubtedly, had his own motives, of which she had been vaguely aware as a child; he would have made her his wife, once she was old enough. But he had been kind to her; he had taught her to read and write, and so many other things. Deep grief assailed her and then she turned cold with sudden fear, hearing the threat, knowing that Fuji would not hesitate to sacrifice Yoshi to gain some advantage for herself. And that Yayoi and Take were no more than pawns in Fuji's game. The safety of all three of them depended on Fuji's silence. But how could she be prevented from betraying them?

※

Yayoi did not have time to reflect more on this disturbing conversation, for her first guest arrived, and then she was kept busy for the rest of the day. Her last visitor was one of her favorites, a merchant from Kitakami. He was no longer young, but not quite middle-aged, the son of an influential family whose specialty was fermentation— soybean products, rice wine, and so on. Their name was Unagi, or Eel, and they guarded carefully both their secret recipes and the contracts they made with farmers all around Lake Kasumi, in which the promise of beans at harvest was exchanged for tools necessary in the planting season, lengths of cloth for summer weddings and festivals, drums for local temples, cord ropes and bamboo baskets.

He lived up to his family name, Yayoi thought, being intelligent, strong, and enterprising, as well as able to slither out of any unpleasant situation. She enjoyed his company as much as his gifts, and the wholehearted pleasure he took in lovemaking reminded her of grilled eel—rich, tasty, good for the health.

But on this day, though they brought considerable pleasure to each other's body, afterward he seemed unusually preoccupied, almost despondent.

"Something is troubling you?" Yayoi said, and called softly to one of the girls to bring more wine.

"Forgive me, Lady Yayoi. I thought I would leave my troubles on the shore, or at least on the boat my servant brought me over on. It's been a strange spring . . . but I don't want to burden you with my problems."

"You can talk to me about anything," Yayoi said. "Even if I can't help, voicing these concerns often clarifies the way you see them."

"Maybe you can help, you are the wisest woman I've ever met. You know my family has been in this business for as long as anyone can remember. We've dealt fairly with people, our house was founded on mutual trust, and that's the way we've always run things. This year more than half of our suppliers have said they can't carry on in the usual way. It appears someone is muscling in on contracts we've had for years, taking them over, blackening our name, and deliberately trying to ruin us. They call themselves the Kikuta—they have been around for some years, though no one seems to know where they came from, but now they have become much more aggressive. The head of the family lets people believe he is Akuzenji's son, though all Akuzenji's children were supposedly killed by Kiyoyori's men years ago."

Yayoi said, "I have never heard of them." She remembered clearly the day Akuzenji died, when she had been so afraid her father would have Shikanoko executed, too.

"We have competitors, naturally, always have had, but this family is different. They use intimidation, and don't hesitate to follow through with their threats, to the point of murder. And not only of farmers but of their wives and children, too. No one dares stand up to them. Now they have started on us, demanding we sell our business, our warehouses, our stock, the vats and all our tools, as well as our secrets, to them. If we don't, they say they will destroy everything and eliminate our family. I didn't take them seriously at first, but now I don't know what to do about it. My father isn't well and I'm afraid the anxiety is going to kill him. I hate to buckle under to bullying, but I have to be realistic."

"What can you do?" Yayoi felt a twinge of unease.

"I am trying to come to some agreement with them. After all, there are precedents—we used to pay Akuzenji to ensure safe transport of our goods overland, and we still employ seamen, who many would describe as pirates, to protect our ships at sea. It's to be expected and saves us keeping a small army of bodyguards. But the Kikuta will not discuss or negotiate; they want complete control. Our only weapon is that they cannot match us for quality, yet. My father has always had the highest standards and he refuses to compromise on that. But even if our buyers are loyal to us, we are falling behind in supplying them because we cannot get our raw ingredients."

Yayoi poured more wine. "Do these people seek to control other merchant houses or only yours?"

"We are the first, I believe," Unagi said, draining the bowl. "However, if we go under, they will start to attack the rest. They treat it like a military campaign. They are the Miboshi with their white banners and we are the red-flagged Kakizuki." He smiled wryly. "And we all know what happened to them! I often wonder if we should not pack up and flee to the west, while we still have the chance."

"But do they ally themselves with the Miboshi? Do they have their support or protection?"

"No, that was just a figure of speech. They ally with no one. But sometimes I feel we are in a kind of war and I must prepare weapons and men. Maybe the Kakizuki should not have fled but fought back, and so should I. That's what my sons want." He sighed. "This isn't what I'd meant to discuss with you tonight. I had another suggestion to put to you."

He took her hand and gazed intently at her face. "I

wish I could bring you with me to Kitakami. I've dreamed of approaching Lady Fuji with an offer. But would you be willing?"

Yayoi was touched and for a moment deeply tempted. She liked and respected Unagi; she knew he would give her a good life.

"Forgive me," he said. "I shouldn't have brought it up at this time. Let me deal with the Kikuta one way or another and then I will speak to Lady Fuji. At least let me know you will consider it."

"I will," she said. "Thank you. I am very grateful."

He stood up. "I will send you a message. Thinking of you is going to give me courage."

He refused Yayoi's offers of food or music, saying he preferred to return to his lodgings before nightfall. She heard the splash of the oar as his servant sculled the boat away.

✻

Yayoi washed and changed her clothes. She took out the Kudzu Vine Treasure Store, intending to study it as she often did at night, but her heart was heavy. The way Unagi had, uncharacteristically, spoken of his problems had unsettled her, and her mind was full of thoughts of the dead. Takaakira must have died years ago, but she had not known of it, and the news had awakened many memories of the past. She had heard snatches of information and gossip on the boats and in the markets, but mostly men came to forget the world of intrigue and strife. If Takaakira had died without her knowing, there was every possibility Shikanoko had, too. She was trapped here in Lady Fuji's world; she would never escape, never find out. Unagi's offer to buy her freedom pulled at her. She tried to imagine for a moment what her life would be like, but she could get no further than the love of a good man, maybe a child, and then she heard Asagao's voice from years ago: *Are they going to marry you to a merchant? What a waste of a beautiful girl!*

She thought how useful she might be to him, since she knew how to write and to calculate. But how far removed it was from her dreams as a child, when she was a warrior's daughter. She wanted to talk it over with Asagao, but it was getting late. *We will talk tomorrow*, she thought, and turned to the text, trying to calm herself in prayer. Whenever she took out the text, she began by meditating on Sesshin, who had given it to her. She did not know if he was alive or dead; she had heard nothing of him since he had been blinded by her stepmother and turned away from Matsutani. She sat motionless, eyes closed, with one hand on the pages.

She felt them rustle, as if a strong wind had suddenly blown through the boat. She opened her eyes and saw for a moment a page that showed the mirrorlike stone. Her hands curved instinctively as if they would clasp it, but then the page turned and, search as she might, she could not find it again.

"Well, I will not read more tonight," she said, almost addressing it as *you wretched book*, trying to control her frustration and disappointment. As she sat back, the pages rustled again. She looked down and saw the text had opened at a place it had never showed her before.

An image leaped out at her. It was a mask, carved from a stag's skull, with antlers. She had seen such things at festivals. Men wore them to dance in, becoming animals or birds, bridging the spaces between the worlds. There were living eyes behind the mask. They looked at her with silent appeal.

"Shikanoko!" she whispered.

But, before she could be sure, the text had closed the page and opened another, showing her a second mask, made from a human skull. Its eyes glittered with gemstones, its lips were painted red, black silky hair had been pasted to the bone. It seemed to turn and look in her direction, as if it were seeking her out. She felt its malevolence and its jealous, restless desire. It was not content with its own power, it could not endure anyone else's but sought to claim all power for itself. With all her effort, she folded the text closed, feeling its resistance, and sat shaking with fear.

What did it mean? Was Shikanoko dead? Or trapped in the world of sorcery, where his mother had warned Yayoi not to follow him? She felt tears forming and struggled not to weep aloud. She remembered so clearly the evening when he had come to tell her about Tsumaru's death. And then she could not keep the tears from falling, recalling her little brother, the last time she had seen him alive, before he had been kidnapped. He had wanted to play with Chika and Kaze, but the other two children had been unwell, and she and Tsumaru had gone out alone into the Darkwood. After that she could only remember the strangers, Tsumaru's cry, her helplessness, her aching head.

Someone called softly, "Hina!" A voice and a name from the past, a whisper, almost lost among the lap of the waves against the side of the boat and the intermittent sound of music. *Hina*, her childhood name, all but forgotten, so long had it been since anyone had used it.

"Hina! Are you awake? I must speak with you."

Wiping her eyes on her sleeve, she hid the Kudzu Vine Treasure Store under a cushion, then lifted the bamboo blind and looked down onto the water. Unagi's narrow skiff was just below, and gripping the side of the pleasure boat to hold it steady was his servant. She had never looked at him closely before, but now, in the light of the lanterns, she recognised him as her childhood companion, the son of Kongyo, one of her father's senior retainers, and of Tsumaru's nurse, Haru.

"Chika? Can it really be you?"

"Can you come down? I need to talk to you."

She pulled a cloth from the rack and wound it around her head and face, then, just as she was, in her nightclothes, climbed over the side and stepped nimbly into the skiff. It rocked and Chika held her to steady her. It was too familiar a touch for a servant and she wondered briefly if she had been wise, trusting a boy she used to play with, now a man, a stranger.

"Don't worry," he said, reading her mind. "I am not going to hurt you or force myself on you. I can't deny I've dreamed you were my wife. I used to imagine we would be married when we were children, playing at being the emperor and the empress. Perhaps we might have been, back then, when we were almost equals. Now I am obliged to work for a merchant and you have ended up a pleasure woman. We have both fallen, but we are further apart than ever."

"The great wheel turns," Yayoi said. "We all rise and fall with it, as we reap the harvest from seeds sown in former lives."

"No," he said. "The harvest we reap is sown by those who wronged us. If neither Heaven nor Earth gives us justice, then we must seek our own revenge."

He helped Yayoi sit in the bow, then took up the single oar at the stern and began to scull. It was a warm evening and the surface of the lake was only slightly ruffled, like twisted silk.

"Unagi is a good man," Yayoi said finally.

"They say he is a good lover," Chika replied.

"That is none of your concern." She heard the bitterness and envy in his voice and pitied him. "How did you come to be in his household, and how did you know me?"

"He talks to me about you—he's not a discreet man, he can't keep his mouth shut—and he mentioned the scroll, the one Master Sesshin gave you that you were always trying to read. I remembered it clearly. Perhaps I was jealous that you should receive such a gift. When I managed to see you for myself, I recognized you." His voice changed slightly, growing more tender. "I had never forgotten you, Hina."

"You should not serve a man you despise," she said, feeling a need to defend Unagi.

"All men despise those they serve," Chika replied, the bitterness returning. "But he is not my true master. I serve him on my master's orders. I will tell you how it all came about. My father died in the battle of Kuromori, and my mother sent my sister and me into the Darkwood. Masachika was searching for anyone who survived, to put them to death. I knew a place where Shikanoko used to live. I took Kaze there."

Yayoi was momentarily deafened by the thump of her own heart. "Was Shikanoko there?"

"No, he has disappeared. People say he is dead, or that he lives the life of a stag, somewhere in the Darkwood." He was silent for a moment, and when he spoke again, his voice was full of contempt. "He ran away. He abandoned us, leaving everyone to die. The only people there were the imps, one of whom I now serve."

"The imps?"

"Lady Tora's children. Do you remember her?"

Yayoi was suddenly cold and nauseated.

"She bewitched your father. It was after she and Shikanoko came to Matsutani that everything started to go wrong. She had five children, all at one time, and they had not one father, but five. One of them was Shikanoko, another Lord Kiyoyori."

"Does that make them brothers to me?"

Chika smiled. "I suppose it does."

While she was absorbing this, he related in a whisper a long account of the brothers, their fathers' names, their magic skills, their use of poisons and venomous creatures, how the Princess died, how they grew as fast as insects and had taken wives, how they had quarreled.

"We returned from Kitakami. Kiku dug up the skull of a man, whom Shikanoko had killed there some time ago, and, with Mu's fox wife, carried out the rituals that have given him such great power."

Yayoi thought, *This is what the book was showing me.* The image of the skull, its searching eyes, made her tremble again. Yet the book must have shown it to her with a purpose, just as it had shown her the stag mask through which shone Shikanoko's eyes.

Chika said, "That is why the brothers are estranged. Mu has many gifts, but now Kiku's are much greater."

"Kiku? Are you talking about the family called Kikuta?"

"That's the name he gave himself when he became a merchant."

My poor Unagi, you are doomed!

"So you are also under his power," she said. "And your sister?"

"Kaze is his wife," Chika replied. "And I am his closest friend, more of a brother than his own siblings. I would do anything for him. He decided I could be an informant and asked me to seek work with Unagi. It was not difficult. I had learned many things from Kiku and I knew how to make myself useful to the house of the Eel. He has come to trust me."

"You will betray him," she said flatly, thinking, *What can I do to prevent that?*

"If I were a servant, it could be called betrayal. But I am a warrior. I have years of disdain and insults to redress."

"Good and evil are not defined by status," Yayoi said.

"You have been sheltered from the world for too long. Everything is defined by status now. Do you think Aritomo does not dispense a different justice to his nobles and lords from that which he metes out to commoners?"

Takaakira's status did not save him, Yayoi thought, but all she said was, "I know very little of Lord Aritomo."

"No doubt he would be very interested to know more about you," Chika said, with a flash of malice.

When Yayoi did not respond, he went on, a little awkwardly, "I do not mean to threaten you."

"I think you do. You have been well taught by your master." She had been fortunate to survive for so long among the riverbank people, but now two people in one day had threatened to expose her. *I must get away. I must warn Yoshi.* But she had no idea how to do either.

Chika said, as though trying to excuse himself, "I was afraid of what Kiku might do to my sister. I had to obey him."

"Why have you come to tell me this?" Yayoi demanded. "What do you want from me?"

He took a deep breath, as though he had finally reached the point of his visit. "Shikanoko possessed a mask, made powerful by the same rituals Kiku used on the skull. After the confrontation with the Prince Abbot, apparently, it became fused to his face. That is why, after the death of the Princess, he fled to the forest, and shuns the company of men and women. I know you are a wise woman, and you have the Kudzu Vine Treasure Store, which must tell you many secrets. Furthermore, my sister had a dream about you, that you put your arms around a stag in the forest, and it turned into a man. I believe you could bring Shikanoko back."

"What are you suggesting? That I go deep into the Darkwood to search for a man who is probably dead, certainly an outlaw?" It was exactly what she longed to do, but surely it was impossible. "You don't understand the circumstances in which I live. I'm not free to come and go as I please."

"You're clever, Hina. You'll find a way. And I'll help you."

Yayoi knew it was unlikely she would be allowed to go anywhere, let alone into the Darkwood on such an illusory mission. She did not trust Chika, suspecting that he, or his master, had other motives to find Shikanoko, and that they would lie to her and try to manipulate her. She remembered the skull's restless searching gaze. But all she could think of was the eyes she had seen behind the mask, their mute appeal, and the dream image of herself, her arms around the stag, her beloved.

❋

She hardly slept. Whenever she closed her eyes she saw the mask. She had short broken dreams in which her hands curved around the stone and she understood everything. During the night she remembered it was the time of year when a few of the acrobats, Yoshi among them,

185

went into the forest to look for young monkeys. The idea came to Yayoi that she might go with them. She knew she was being foolish, that the Darkwood was vast, that she was familiar with only the tiny southwestern corner of it, but she was impelled by a belief that fate would bring her to him, wherever he was and in whatever form. And, in the Darkwood, she would find a way to warn Yoshi not to return.

For years she had done nothing without Lady Fuji's permission. She tried to plan how best to approach her, but, as she had feared, Fuji's instant reaction was a refusal.

"It is our busiest time of year; the fine weather, the summer festivals, all the extra gifts that will need to be recorded. It is very selfish of you even to think of such a thing. Whatever reason can you have for wanting to traipse through the forest with the monkey boys?"

"I am a little tired," Yayoi said, fanning herself. "I feel jaded. I will be better for a short break from entertaining."

"Well, we will go on a pilgrimage somewhere in the autumn." Fuji was looking at her shrewdly. "There is some other reason, I feel. Are you planning to run away with one of our clients? It's Unagi, isn't it?"

"In truth, Unagi said last night he would like me to go with him, but naturally he would approach you first. I am wondering whether to encourage him or not. Some time away will help me think clearly. And I thought I might call in at the convent. I would like to see the Abbess again."

"Whatever for? You can't go back, Yayoi. If you want to bury your past you must bury all of it. And put all thoughts of Unagi out of your mind. He is not as rich as he once was and he can't afford you. No, it is quite impossible!" She began to fan herself vigorously.

They were sitting in the stern of the boat. It was still early morning, but the sky was already an intense blue and the sun was hot. A shade awning protected them, but Yayoi could feel the sweat gathering on her skin. The water was green and clear. She longed to lower herself into it. She felt a sudden wave of fury that she was not allowed to act as she wished, that she would always be trapped by Fuji, always afraid that the woman would betray her and Yoshi. She pressed her lips together, not daring to let any words escape her, wishing with all her heart that Fuji were dead.

There was a small splash and a ripple of movement. They both looked over the side of the boat. Far below a shadow flickered across the lake floor.

"It is just a water rat," Fuji said. "Come, enough sitting around. We must get ready for the day."

But Yayoi knew the creature underwater was too large to be a rat. She followed the ripple with her eyes and thought she saw a reed moving through the water.

❄

Fuji died that night. It had been a busy day, with many visitors. Yayoi had entertained three of her special guests and had then played with the musicians until her fingers were stiff and her head ached. She had fallen asleep soon after the moon had risen, and had been woken at dawn, while the moon was still high in the sky, by the shocked cries and wailing of Fuji's maid.

She ran immediately to the lifeless body, slapped her cheeks, rubbed her wrists and ankles, burned incense under her nose, called her name repeatedly, but no breath returned. Fuji, so healthy and lively the night before, had departed on her final journey.

There were no marks on her body, no external wounds. Her mouth smelled faintly sweetish and Yayoi guessed she must have been poisoned, though by whom, or for what reason, no one could fathom.

The boats left at once for Aomizu. They were supposed to be heading for Kitakami, for the twenty-fifth-day market, but that would have to be canceled. The funeral had to be held quickly, because of the intense heat, and the speed of it all somehow increased the shock and disbelief. But Yayoi noticed that, despite their shared grief, the other women and the musicians were wary of her and talked about her when they thought she could not hear.

The following day, Takemaru came to the boat, calling out to her from the shore, addressing her as Older Sister. She knew that he was uncomfortable on the boats, that the pleasures of love both attracted and repelled him. He was at that age, confused by desire and emotion, happiest in the company of boys his own age and the young men whom he admired excessively, yet drawn to girls. Soon, she knew, one of the women would find it entertaining to take him behind the bamboo blinds and initiate him, and then he would probably lose his mind and be insatiable for a couple of years. It amused and saddened her at the same time. She did not expect, now, to have children herself. Take was both younger brother and son to her.

He was a tall, well-built boy—too tall to be an acrobat, the others said, when they wanted to annoy him, but they could not deny that his strength made him useful, as a baseman, in the living towers they created of humans and monkeys. Already, he could take the weight of the older men on his shoulders or on his upturned feet. He was quick-tempered, bold, and determined in nature; if he could not conquer something he practiced obsessively until he could do it perfectly. He loved listening to tales of warriors of old, their battles, their victories and defeats, and often played with a wooden pole as if it were a sword or a spear. The acrobats teased Take for his bloodthirsty and violent games, but Yayoi, who knew his parentage, saw in him Shikanoko's warrior traits as well as Akihime's nobility and courage.

The drummer girl, Kai, was with him. Yayoi had never been close to her. They had almost instinctively stayed away from each other, as though knowing they had overlapping secrets that they did not dare reveal. Because of some slight deformity, Kai had never joined the pleasure women on the boats but had been brought up by the musicians. Yayoi had seen her tiny shell-shaped ears once or twice when the wind blew her hair away from her face. Yet Yoshi had fallen in love with her; they were as good as married. Yayoi could not help feeling a pang of regret and envy.

She took her sandals in her hand, and a parasol to protect her face from the sun's glare, and crossed to the shore. It was a relief to get away from the sobbing women—and from some other oppressive, disturbing feeling, some accusation in their eyes and the way they fell silent at her approach.

Kai greeted her warmly and the three of them walked to the end of the dock.

Take said, "They are saying you killed Lady Fuji."

"How can anyone believe that? Of course I did not!" *Yet*, Yayoi thought, *I wished her dead.*

"You were the last person to see her alive," Kai said, "and you know magic arts, fatal ones. They are saying you cast a spell on her because she would not grant your request."

"Where did you hear this?" Yayoi asked.

"Gossip in town," Take replied. "Yoshimaru told us."

"Does Yoshi believe it?"

"No, of course not, and nor do Kai and I. But he thinks you should come away with us, in case some official hears the rumors and decides to act on them."

"If I run away, I will be confirming their suspicions," Yayoi said.

"Older Sister, only you can decide what is best; you are wiser than any of us. We are leaving directly for the forest. I was coming to say goodbye. Get what you want to bring, don't tell anyone, just say you are walking to the crossroads with Kai to bid us farewell."

"You have thought it all out," she whispered.

"Yoshi told me what to say," he admitted.

Yoshi. Fuji had threatened to turn him over to Lord Aritomo, to expose who Yayoi really was, and then had tried to prevent her from leaving. She felt a pang of guilt. Even though she had not killed Fuji, there was no doubt she was going to benefit from her death. Was it a miracle from Heaven, or had it been the creature that was not a water rat, Chika, his mysterious master, or someone else from the Kikuta tribe?

"I will accompany you a little way," she said in a louder voice. "Just wait a moment."

She knew she must act. She would never have another opportunity like this. She had to find Shikanoko, take Yoshimori to him, so that the true heir of the previous emperor could be restored to the throne. And she had to give Shikanoko his son, Take.

She went back to the boat and collected a few things together, the Kudzu Vine Treasure Store among them. She did not dare take too much; she left her writing implements and her clothes. She was just tying the corners of the carrying cloth when a shadow fell against the blind and a voice called quietly, "Yayoi!"

It was Asagao, the only person Yayoi could call a friend, apart from Bara, who had been her maid long ago and whom she remembered vaguely but fondly. She and Asagao were close in age, had slept side by side when they were children, hidden away in the women's temple, had caressed and kissed each other when they had begun to learn about love. They had laughed over the ridiculous men who fell in love with them, shed tears for the charming ones who would wed other ordinary women, nursed each other in sickness, bled every month on the same days.

"Are you leaving?" Asagao said.

"No, I am just walking with Kai as far as the crossroads." It pained Yayoi to lie to her, so she said no more.

"It isn't true, is it, what people are saying?" Asagao was watching her closely.

"No," she said simply.

"But you are not grieving. You have hardly shed a tear. You might not have killed her, but you are not sorry she is dead."

"I am grieving. I just find it hard to express my feelings, you know that." Yayoi strove to keep her voice light and natural.

"Yes, Yayoi, you keep everything hidden, even from your friend," Asagao replied.

Yayoi tied the last knot and lifted the bundle.

Asagao said, "What about the lute? Aren't you taking that?"

"Why should I? I will be back very soon." Yayoi hated leaving Genzo, but she did not dare take it, for it had no guile. It would begin to play in Yoshi's presence and betray him.

"Can I play it?" Asagao asked.

"Of course, but it is not easy."

"I will look after it for you."

Yayoi looked at her and saw she had not convinced her. She took her in her arms and whispered, "Goodbye."

"Don't leave. Why do you have to go? What am I going to do without you?"

"I'm sorry. I can't explain."

Asagao began to weep and Yayoi felt her own eyes moisten in sympathy. She could think of nothing else to say. She knew only that she had to take this chance and leave now, before it was too late. She joined Take and Kai on the shore and walked away from the pleasure boats, which had been her life for so many years.

11

CHIKA

Chika returned to Kitakami and immediately went to the merchant house, which was now the center of the Kikuta empire, and his home. Kiku was overseeing the sampling of the latest batch of soy bean paste. His eyes lit up when Chika came in, and he handed his ladle over to the nearest servant and took Chika into the back room, which overlooked the port, the estuary, and the vast expanse of the Northern Sea.

"Lady Hina has left?" he asked eagerly.

"Yes, she has gone to the Darkwood with the monkey acrobats."

"Were there any problems?"

"Fuji was going to prevent her, so . . ."

"So you very cleverly killed her, leaving no trace?"

Chika nodded.

"Kuro has taught you something after all. Come here. You did well."

Around him Chika could hear the sounds of the vats being weighed down with stones, to bring the soybeans to fermentation. The smell was intense, making the days of high summer seem even hotter. From the shop, he could hear his sister's voice, greeting customers, giving orders to other women, scolding the children. It should have annoyed him—after all, she was a warrior's daughter, she should not have ended up a merchant's wife, especially when that merchant was not even fully human. Yet he did not refuse to approach Kiku, and allowed the other man to embrace him, feeling the familiar stab of desire, all the stronger for being tinged with repulsion. No one else, since his father died, had met his need for approval and love, and Kiku still fascinated him, as he had since the first day Chika had spied on the boys at the hermit sorcerer's place in the forest and seen how they could split into two separate selves and fade into invisibility. He had been following the monk Gessho, had watched the fight in which both the monk and the sorcerer died, and had longed to be like those boys, to have such skills.

He had learned everything Kiku and Kuro could teach him, but some things could not be taught. They were innate skills and could not be acquired. His nephews and nieces possessed them in varying degrees. He had watched them develop, as the children grew, envious of them and delighted by them at the same time. There were a lot of children. Kiku had restrained his pleasure in killing to some extent, but not his lust. Chika's sister, Kaze, seemed always to be pregnant, as were the female servants. Kuro was the same, fathering many children, a couple of whom he brought home in a basket, handing them over without explanation to Kaze to bring up. Even Ku had found a wife and started a family.

The brothers liked the children, almost to excess, Chika thought. It surprised him, for in all other matters they showed little gentleness and no sentimentality. The children were precocious, walking at six months, talking before they were a year old, but they matured more slowly than their fathers, due to their mothers' human blood.

"There is no one like us," Kiku often said. "We have to make our own tribe." More and more frequently he referred to the three linked families in that fashion, and soon they were all calling themselves the Tribe.

Sometimes Chika envied them. If his life had not been disrupted by war, he would be married, with children of his own. But who would he marry now? He was no longer a warrior, yet he was not really anything else. Outside the Tribe he had no caste or family, yet he would never be truly one of them. He thought of Hina, as he often did, recalling her beauty and charm. *She could have been mine. What would our children be like?* The idea that Unagi hoped to take her as his wife enraged and saddened him, as did the realization that Hina loved Shikanoko. He had seen it in her face when he had told her of his sister's dream.

One is a merchant, one an outlaw, yet they both have more chance of winning her than I do, he reflected.

Now Kiku said, still holding him close, "You and

your sister have made me more human. You came to me when I needed to learn how to relate to other people. We were the same age. I know that warriors, like the family you came from, feel strong bonds of loyalty. While I am not sure I fully understand that idea, I do feel a bond with you. I will always be grateful for that."

"I owe you everything," Chika replied. "And yes, there is a bond between us."

Kiku said, "I used to watch the fake wolf, the one that attached itself to Shika—did you ever see it?"

"Once, at Matsutani," Chika replied. "And of course during the winter he spent at Kumayama it was always at his heels."

"Affection made it become more real—it grew and changed, in a way the other animals Shisoku created could not. I often wonder what he did, when he made that one, that enabled it to love and so to grow. Do you suppose it has died, as a real wolf would have done by now, or has its artificiality extended its life?"

"With luck, we will find out before too long," Chika said.

Kiku smiled as he released him. "I hope so."

"What do you want me to do now?" Chika said.

"It is the mask that gives Shika such great power. As we know, it cannot now be taken from his face. But like my skull it was created through combining male and female essences. I've learned from Akuzenji's sorcerers that in such circumstances the mask can only be removed by a woman who loves him. You told me before, after Kaze's dream, that Hina might be that woman."

"I'm sure of it now," Chika said, after a moment.

"You are jealous, Chika?" Kiku said with his customary acute perception. "Do you want her for your wife?"

"Maybe I do. Maybe I always have."

"Your family have significant dreams," Kiku said. "What about your father? Didn't he have a dream about Shika, that he straddled the realm, holding power in one hand and the Emperor in the other?"

"My father believed it was a prophecy," Chika said. "But Shikanoko rejected the opportunity to take power when it was offered to him."

Kiku said slowly, "The Princess's death affected him so strongly."

"If my sister died," Chika said, "would you walk away from your little empire, from all you have built up?"

Kiku stared at him, trying to fathom the meaning behind the question. "Probably not," he admitted. "Though I am very fond of her, in the same way I am fond of you. But all that happened years ago. Surely Shika will have recovered from grief by now."

"There are some things we never recover from," Chika replied.

Kiku said, "That is hard for me to understand. The thing is, I really *need* the mask, with or without Shika." He smiled, with the small gratification of using an exact word whose meaning had never been clear to him till now. "If Hina cannot remove it, we will take it, still attached to his head. He turned us away. 'Let me never set eyes on you again,' he said. Once he is dead, you can have Hina."

"He betrayed many," Chika said, "when he did not return to Kumayama. I'll never forget those who died as a result, and I'll never forgive him. It will be a pleasure to kill him."

Kiku turned pale, and for a moment did not respond. Then he seemed to gather himself together. "It disturbs me to talk of killing him," he said. "I am very confused. Sometimes I hate him, sometimes I feel another kind of emotion. I long to see him again." He struck his chin with his fist two or three times. "It is as if something is driving me to confront him, almost as if the skull wants to challenge the mask. I will have no rest until I hold it in my hands."

After a few moments of silence, Chika said, "So I am to go after Hina and take her to Shikanoko, and once he is released from the mask—what then? Do you want me to kill him or not?"

"I cannot decide," Kiku said. "I must give it more thought. Maybe you should go first to my brothers Ima and Mu. I have been thinking for some time that we five were born together—we should all live together, all five families. Only Mu fully understands Kuro and myself. Tell him I want to see him. I want us to work together."

"You will have to apologize to him and beg his forgiveness," Chika said. "You tied him up and slept with his wife. Most people would consider that a terrible betrayal."

"She was a fox woman," Kiku said, "less human than I am."

"Mu loved her deeply, though," Chika said.

Kiku shifted uncomfortably. "Maybe I envied that, being able to love."

"That's why you have to ask him to forgive you."

"That word again," Kiku said. "What does it mean?"

"That you are sorry you hurt him."

Kiku scowled. "Very well. Tell him I am sorry."

"Deeply sorry."

"Whatever you like," Kiku said, with a flash of impatience. "Whatever it takes."

12

HINA (YAYOI)

Kai did not turn back at the crossroads but walked on alongside Yoshi, her drum slung across her back. From time to time she brought it forward and sent its dull note reverberating through the trees. She laughed and chattered with Yoshi and Saru. Yayoi remembered how Fuji had told her that Kai and Yoshi had been taken onto the boat at the same time. Now she wondered how much Kai remembered of her previous life, and what she knew of Yoshi. Watching them together, she became aware of a deep understanding between them, the sort that people described as a bond from a former life.

From time to time she caught a glimpse of the bird that always followed Yoshi. Yayoi had long suspected it was a werehawk, like the one that had flown to Matsutani, the day the bandits were captured. Shikanoko had killed it with an arrow when no one else had been able to. It was many years ago, yet she still remembered vividly the creature plummeting to the ground, its blood sizzling, Shikanoko's stance, her father's expression.

That bird had been completely black, apart from its yellow eyes, but this one had a spangling of gold, as though its plumage were changing color from year to year. It did not seem to age or suffer. Yoshi did not care for it; he never fed it or spoke to it, yet he sometimes referred to it by its name: Kon. Kai was kind to it, as she was to all birds. It was obvious to Yayoi that, like Genzo, Kon knew the young acrobat's true identity. Together with Kai, they were all that remained of Yoshi's former life, a link with the past that he did not—or did not want to—remember. She had left the lute with Asagao, but Kon chose where he went and whom he followed.

"Sometimes they try to trap him," Take told her, following her gaze. "Yoshi would love it if he stayed home in a cage. But he is too clever to be caught. I have offered to try to shoot him down, but of course they would not allow him to be killed."

Yayoi knew the open secret that the acrobats all belonged to a sect, a kind of hidden religion, that forbade the taking of any life. There was some divine mother and child they worshipped, which she often thought must be the reason they loved children, and remained in some ways children themselves. She was also aware that they always sought a blessing before going on a journey, and that a priest of the sect lived not far from Aomizu, so she was not altogether surprised when, late in the first day, in silent agreement, Yoshi and Saru took a side track that led away to the north.

They took one monkey with them to entice the wild ones they hoped to capture to replace Yoshi's two companions, Kemuri and Shiro, who had both died the previous winter. Saru's favorite, Tomo, had died the year before. This monkey was a young one, captured in the forest two summers earlier. They called it Noboru. Saru led it by a long red cord, and when it was tired it sat on his shoulders. They also had one packhorse, carrying their provisions and empty baskets for the new monkeys. Toward the end of the day, Yayoi sat on the horse, perched between the baskets. The acrobats were tireless, but it was a long time since she had walked anywhere and her legs were aching. The packhorse plodded, stumbling frequently. She wished she could put on leggings and ride as she had when she was a child, astride, freely.

After more than three hours, when it was almost dark, they came to a tiny village, four or five huts huddled together at the foot of a tall hill, almost a true mountain. The way was overgrown and led through thick groves of trees and clumps of bamboo. Every now and then, Yoshi and Saru removed, and replaced behind them, the brushwood that had been laid across the path.

It must be a love of secrecy for its own sake, Yayoi thought, for she did not believe there was any real danger of attack. Many sects had sprung up in the years of difficulty and famine, as people sought to understand Heaven's hostility and placate it. Some were followers of the Enlightened One who taught a new, austere path, others turned to the old gods of mountain and forest. Unless they caused riots and disturbed the civil peace, they were allowed to flourish, especially if they paid contributions to Lord Aritomo's system of taxation.

The old man came out to greet them, as happy as a father meeting his children again after a long absence. A meal was quickly prepared, taro with millet, flavored with the dried seaweed Saru had brought as a gift, followed by mulberries and loquats, picked from the trees that surrounded the small fields. Before they ate, the old man prayed over the food, speaking a blessing on the visitors and on their journey.

When he came to Yayoi he said quietly, "You have not been here before, but you are welcome. What is your reason for traveling to the Darkwood?"

"I hope to gather herbs of healing," she said. "There are many that can be found nowhere else."

"Use them only for good," he said. "Beware of being led into sorcery. And turn to the Secret One, for he is the source of true healing."

She bowed her head, saying nothing, but she couldn't help glancing at the others. Yoshi's eyes were closed and his face calm and rapt. *All this has so much meaning for him*, she thought. *He believes with all his heart. But the emperor is called upon to carry out rituals that bind Heaven and Earth. How would he be able to do that? Better he remains undiscovered and lives out his life among the acrobats.*

She prayed now, to any god that might listen, that Fuji had not had time to report her suspicions of Yoshi before her death, that they would not be pursued, that Yoshi would be able to return at the end of the summer, and then she regretted her presumption in daring to suggest that the powers of Heaven might be turned from their purpose. He was the Emperor. He could not avoid his destiny, or the sacrifices that would be demanded of him.

The sparse food and the turmoil of her thoughts gave her a restless night. For a long time she lay, eyes wide open, alongside the women and their children, dozed eventually, and awoke at dawn. When she went outside Kon was calling quietly from the roof, and Take was standing at the entrance to the path, as if on guard, his staff in his hand.

"Have you been keeping watch all night?" she asked.

"I slept for a couple of hours. Then I dreamed Kon was speaking to me, some urgent message. It woke me up and I came outside. There is some danger, I can feel it."

"Do you think we are being followed?" Yayoi felt her world shrink again, as though she had just escaped from prison, only to be recaptured.

He gave her a measured look, mature beyond his years. "Yoshi and Saru aren't worried. They believe, since they threaten no one, no one will threaten them. But someone could be following us—maybe the authorities investigating Fuji's death, or maybe . . ."

Lord Arinori, my so-called protector, who, if he is not going to have me executed for murder, might seek to own me completely, or Chika or his master and his brothers.

"What should we do?" she said.

"We are safer here than on the road. We should stay for a few days. I'll see what news I can discover and return by nightfall. Tell the others where I've gone and wait for me here."

She tried to persuade him not to go alone, but he was impatient and would not countenance any opposition to his plan. He set out at once before the others woke, leaving Yayoi to explain where he had gone.

Saru and Yoshi mocked his concerns but were happy to spend at least one more day with their beloved teacher. Take returned in the late afternoon, looking pleased with himself.

"I was right," he whispered to Yayoi. "Someone did come after you—Lord Arinori."

She felt a jolt of fear. If they had stayed on the road, he would have caught up with them.

"It's a good thing I stuck to my decision. He has gone to the temple where you lived for a while. He thinks you would have fled there. We will stay a few more days until he has returned to Aomizu."

She remembered the earlier search at the temple, the destruction, the nuns' terror.

"Don't worry," Take said, seeing her expression. "If he does not find you there, what will he do? He is not going to hurt the nuns."

Yayoi gave her fine robes to the village women, telling them to get rid of them or sell them at the market. She dressed in the dull, shabby clothes of a peasant, and worked alongside the women in the fields, letting the earth stain her hands and the sun darken her skin. The young men cut wood for the winter, helped build a new shed to stack it in. There was always work to do and the villagers were grateful for the extra hands. Many days passed before they were ready to move on. They laughed at the dangers that Take saw everywhere, his mind influenced by the tales and legends of the past that he so loved, their intrigues, betrayals, battles, and uprisings, and teased him until he lost his temper.

The morning they left, they knelt before the old man to say goodbye and receive his blessing.

He smiled when he looked down at Saru. "May you find a friend to replace the one you lost." To Kai he said, "I am glad you are staying here with us. You and your child will be safe here."

Kai smiled, blushing a little, and reached out to touch Yoshi's hand. He grinned, too, but the old man turned to him with a somber face. "What you seek will not be found in the Darkwood. It is not what you think, maybe not even what you desire. I told you once, all paths lead to your destiny."

"Master your anger," he said to Take. "It blinds you to what is real and what is best for you."

To Yayoi, he said, "You may use your real name now. Your old life is finished." And from that moment she called herself Hina again.

❋

Take hurried them off the track, as soon as possible, and they began to make their way eastward, meeting the road to Shimaura some way south of the crossroads where the highway from Aomizu went on to Rinrakuji. They slept for a short time on the edge of the fields, and were woken in the early morning by two small boys who demanded to see the monkey.

"Wait a few months and we will be back with a whole troupe," Saru promised.

They walked all day, and then took a track that turned off to the east. The two young men and Take had been here many times, but for Hina it was completely new. The forest closed around them. Cicadas shrilled in a constant shower of sound and mosquitoes whined. The air was stifling, the track stony. For a while she rode the horse, but it stumbled often, its straw shoes slipping on the rocky ground, and she felt safer walking.

She thought they would sleep in the open air again, but in the late afternoon she saw they were approaching a derelict hut. Take had gone ahead to scout, and came running back.

"There are people in the hut," he said in a loud whisper.

Hina stopped, Yoshi beside her.

"I don't like this place," Yoshi said. "I've been past it many times, and it always makes me tremble."

"Did something bad happen here?" she asked.

His face closed and she knew she was right, but he would never tell her.

Saru, with the horse and Noboru the monkey, went blithely on, calling out a greeting.

There was a slight noise from inside and a tall woman stepped out, holding a broken plank of wood in both hands, as if it were a club, a look of fear on her face. Her head was shaved, her tattered robe a dull brown color.

Hina thought she recognized her but could not believe it was the same woman. Was it a ghost or an illusion? "Reverend Nun?" she questioned, walking forward.

Astonishment, then anger, replaced fear as the woman lowered the plank. "You are one of Lady Fuji's girls. The one we called Yayoi. What are you doing here? It is on your account that all these disasters came upon us. What have you done?"

"What happened?" Hina said.

The monkey was screaming loudly from Saru's shoulder and showing its teeth. The nun looked at it, and then back at Hina. She swayed slightly. The plank dropped from her hands. She crouched down, her face in her palms, her shoulders heaving.

Hina knelt in front of her, the others waiting a few paces behind; Yoshi and Saru silent and concerned, Take turning constantly, his eyes raking the forest and the track they had come along, as if suspecting a trap. There was a clatter of wings and Kon alighted on the roof. It called in its fluting voice, silencing the birds of the forest. In this hush, a voice came from inside.

"Who is there?"

Hina would never forget that voice. "It is the Abbess," she whispered. The nun nodded, without speaking.

"Shall I go in to her?"

Take rushed forward. "It may be a trap. Let me go."

"There is no one inside but our lady," the nun said, her voice hoarse with tears.

Nevertheless, Take, holding the pole ready, stepped inside. Hina followed him. There was no door—it had warped and fallen years before—and the hut smelled of damp and mildew and of something else, a sweetish, stomach-turning whiff of flesh rotting.

"She's telling the truth," Take said. He moved back to the door as Hina went forward and knelt beside the small figure lying on the ground. She was about to take one of the Abbess's hands, when her eyes adjusted to the gloom and she saw the injuries.

The skin had been seared away. The flesh was raw and swollen. Yellow and black streaks of infection ran up both arms. The fingers were turning dark.

"It is Hina," she said softly. "I used to be called Yayoi. I lived at the temple."

"Yayoi, dear child," the Abbess said. Her voice was calm and clear, despite the fever. "Look at what has become of me! I am dying, but I am glad to see you. Heaven has sent you to me."

"What happened to you?" Hina said. "Who did this to you?"

"I did it to myself, foolish old woman that I am. Lord Arinori came to the temple again. This time he was looking for you. Of course, I did not know where you were, nor had I heard the news of Fuji's death. I could tell him nothing. He became very angry when none of his threats worked on us, and had his men set fire to the building. My little cat—you probably knew her mother—was trapped inside. I tried to save her, but the flames were too fierce. Poor creature, she was the victim of human rage and hatred, and I was punished for my stupid, vain attachment."

"Don't blame yourself," Hina said. "Blame the cruelty of men."

"Men will always be cruel and destructive," the Abbess said. "We live with that as we live with typhoons and earthquakes. I could not reach my cat, but I was able to snatch one object from the flames. Now you are here, I understand it was for you. It is by my side. Can you see it?"

Hina groped around with her hands in the half darkness and came upon what felt like a smooth, rounded stone. Her palms seemed to recognize it and it knew them in return, nestling into them. She lifted it and held it up so the Abbess could see it.

"Is this it?"

"Yes."

Hina peered at it. It gleamed slightly even in the gloom inside the hut. It was reflective, like a mirror. She could almost see her face in it.

"It is a medicine stone," the Abbess said. "I knew it was for you when you came to the temple with the Kudzu Vine Treasure Store—do you still have it?"

"I do," Hina said. "I left almost everything else behind, but the text I brought with me."

A smile flitted over the Abbess's face. "The stone and the text belong together. I should have given it to you then, but you were only a child, and you seemed destined for another kind of life. Now you are here, like a miracle. I can only conclude the stone brought you here so you could be united."

"What is it for?" Hina asked.

"Hold it to my mouth so it catches my breath."

Hina did so and a mist covered the polished surface.

"Now look deeply into it," the Abbess said.

Hina could not help crying out.

"What did you see?"

"I cannot say!"

"Say it," the Abbess commanded her. "I am not afraid. It revealed I am dying, didn't it?"

Hina found she could not put into words what the stone had shown her: the intricate workings of the body, all failing one after another, before the inexorable invasion that was death. Tears formed in her eyes and she wept for the incurable frailty of the human body, its passage from birth and growth to decay and death, through a brief moment of passionate, striving life.

"It will show you the fate of any sick person," the Abbess said. "Whether they will recover or if they should prepare themselves to cross the three-streamed river of death. To most people it will seem like a dull black stone. Only in cases of imminent death does it reveal itself to be a mirror."

Her calmness added to the awe Hina felt for the magical object in her hands. She put it down carefully, leaned over the older woman, and placed her hand on the burning forehead.

"Your hands are so cool," the Abbess said. Her eyes closed and she seemed to sleep for a few moments. Then she said, "Where are you going?"

Hina said, "I am going into the Darkwood to find Shikanoko."

"Shikanoko, the outlaw?"

"Your son. You called him Kazumaru. I don't believe he became a monster, as you feared."

"So you are going in search of him?" the Abbess said wonderingly. "He has been much on my mind, as I lie here, dying. Why are you looking for him? Is it because you love him? But how can that be? You can't have been much more than a child when you knew him, if you knew him at all . . ." Her speech became more rambling and incoherent and Hina could not follow everything she said. She was afraid the end was near, and was about to call the nun, when the dying woman spoke more clearly. "When you find him, tell him his mother forgives him."

"Maybe you should ask him to forgive you," Hina said. "If you had not left him when he was a child . . . I am sorry, it is none of my concern." But then she felt strongly that it was her concern, and her anger and pity rushed to the surface. "You abandoned him! That is what made him become a sorcerer."

There was a long silence. She feared the Abbess had stopped breathing and leaned over her to check. The woman raised her head toward her and spoke with surprising force. "You are right. I see it all so clearly now. I thought I was seeking holiness. I so wanted to be good. But in the end I gave my cat more affection than I ever gave my son, and for that I am dying." Her voice was filled with despair and bitterness.

She must not die like this, after a whole life dedicated to the sacred, Hina thought. Take had remained on the

213

threshold while they had been talking. Now Hina turned to him. She had not intended to tell him who his father was until they found Shikanoko—for all her confident words, she could not know what he might have become, what grief and loneliness might have wrought in him. She might never find him; she might find a monster. But she had to let Take meet his grandmother, now fate had brought them so close.

"Take," she called softly, "come here!"

He knelt beside them, his eyes widening in pity as he saw the damaged hands.

"You know her?" he said. "Who is she, poor lady?"

"She is the abbess of the temple where I lived for some years, after you and I were rescued from the lake. And she is your grandmother."

The Abbess's eyelids had closed, but now they flew open and she searched for Take's face. "Who is this boy?" she whispered.

"He is called Takeyoshi. He is Shikanoko's son. His mother was Akihime, the Autumn Princess. He is your grandson."

"Is it true?" the Abbess said, and Take echoed her with the same words, as their eyes locked.

"It is true," Hina said.

Tears flowed from the Abbess's eyes. "I want to touch his face, stroke his hair, but I cannot bear the pain."

Take put his own hand to her face and wiped away the tears with his fingers.

"When you find your father, ask him to forgive me," she said.

She did not speak again. Her face took on a calm and joyful expression. Little by little the smell of sickness abated and was replaced by a fragrance like jasmine.

Hina found her lips repeating one of the sutras, that she had chanted so many times at the temple, that she had read aloud to the Abbess, as her tears fell for the dying woman.

The nun came in and joined in the chanting. The hut seemed to glow with light.

"The Enlightened One is coming for her," the nun whispered. "He will take her straight to Paradise."

The Abbess began to breathe rapidly. Her eyelids fluttered. She seemed to want to speak, or maybe she was praying. Then the quick breaths ceased in one last sigh. Her eyes opened, but they no longer looked on this world.

Kon called piercingly and the monkey, Noboru, screeched in response.

The nun said, "The other nuns went to Rinrakuji, to get help. They will be back soon. I'll stay with her body, but you should not linger here. Rinrakuji is a Miboshi temple now. I don't know what you are supposed to have done, or who you really are, but you don't want to get embroiled in their questions and their procedures."

"What will happen to you?" Hina said.

"They will no doubt find a place for us, washing dishes, sweeping floors. There are many ways a nun can serve."

"But you have had your own temple, free from the control of men! You will find it hard to serve them now."

"It could not last," the nun said in a resigned voice. "All over the country, men are gaining power over women. They are in the ascendant, and will be for years to come. Women are condemned to begin their decline. It is all one, part of the great cycle."

Hina knelt to ask for her blessing and Take imitated her. Then they bowed in farewell to the corpse and left the hut, Hina clasping the stone.

Once outside Take turned to her, his eyes bright with unshed tears.

"Tell me everything."

"I will," she replied, with a swift glance at Yoshi, who was waiting with Saru, both sitting on their haunches. The monkey was on Saru's shoulder, searching his hair for fleas. The horse was cropping grass at the edge of the stream. "But not now. Later, when we are alone, I promise."

"What's happening?" Saru said. "Are we stopping here for the night?"

"What's the matter with you?" Yoshi said to Take. "Is something wrong?"

"A woman died in there," Hina said.

Both young men drew the cross sign in the air.

"Let's get going, then," Saru said with a nervous laugh. "I'm not all that fond of the dead."

"Shouldn't we help bury her?" Yoshi said.

"People will be coming soon," Hina said. "Really, it's best if we leave without delay."

Take seemed about to speak, but Hina shook her head at him. He ran to the stream, surprised the horse with a whack on its rump, jumped from rock to rock, and disappeared into the forest. The horse flung up its head and galloped after him. The others had to follow.

✳

They walked until well after nightfall, the three-quarters moon of the seventh month lighting their path, and slept briefly on the ground until the forest birds began to call before dawn.

Yoshi and Saru went on ahead, but Take, alongside Hina, walked more and more slowly until they were a long distance behind.

"I thought my father must have been a warrior," he said, when the others were out of earshot. "It would explain so much about me. But what else do you know about my parents?"

She told him all she remembered from her childhood, the day Shikanoko arrived on the brown mare, his unparalleled skill with the bow, how he brought down the Prince Abbot's werehawk and had been able to ride the stallion Nyorin, which no one else could, after the death of its master, Akuzenji.

"He was born at Kumayama, and is the true heir to that estate. It lies a little farther to the east from my father's twin estates of Matsutani and Kuromori."

"Kuromori? The Darkwood?"

"Yes."

Take gestured at the huge forest through which they were walking, the mossy trunks, the twisted roots, the fern-fringed streambeds. "So all this was your father's?"

"If the Darkwood belonged to anyone, it was to him. But we lived on the southwestern corner. All this part is completely wild."

"What happened to your father?" Take asked.

"He died at the side of the Crown Prince, along with your other grandfather, Hidetake, in the Ninpei rebellion."

Take absorbed this silently, glancing at Hina with new concern. She wondered how much he had heard of the legends, rumors, and ballads that had sprung up around Lord Kiyoyori and his son, the dragon child, and what he knew of the struggle between the Miboshi and the Kakizuki.

"Who owns the Darkwood now?" he said. "Weren't you his heir?"

"My uncle, Masachika. He had been sent to join the Miboshi when he was a young man, so he ended up on the side of the victors. He thinks I am dead, and must never find out otherwise. It was he who came to Nishimi and discovered the Princess, your mother, hiding there, not long after you were born. That's when I ran away with you, and the acrobats rescued us."

"Did he kill her?" Hina saw in his face that he was already thinking of revenge.

"Not directly. He had her transported to Miyako and she died there."

"And my father—what is his name?" he said after a long silence.

"Shikanoko. He was always called just that. It means the deer's child."

"Is he still alive?"

"It seems so, for they are searching for him. Unless he died in the Darkwood. But, as I told the Abbess—I don't know if you heard—I am also looking for him."

"My grandmother," he stated. "The first of my family I have ever met, and then she died within moments. I lay awake all night, thinking of her, praying for her soul."

"Yes, I did, too," Hina replied.

They walked on slowly. Yoshi and Saru were out of sight ahead, but from time to time they heard Kon calling and Noboru chattering.

"A little while ago," Hina said, thinking she should explain her reasons more fully, "a man came to visit me. I knew him when we were children. He was the son of my father's senior retainer, and the same age as me. After my father's death he fell on hard times, but was taken in by a man who has become powerful in the north, in Kitakami. This man and his brothers were the children of a woman who came to our house at the same time as Shikanoko. She bewitched my father and he fell in love with her."

She was surprised how hard it was to say this. Her face was burning.

"They are his children? Your brothers?" Take said, puzzled.

"There was some sorcery at work. They were all born at one time, they had several men for their fathers. My father was one, Shikanoko another."

"So they are my brothers, too?"

"In a way, yes." She did not want to tell him everything she had learned from Chika, how the brothers had gone with Shikanoko to Ryusonji and caused the Princess's death. "This man, my childhood friend, Chika, begged me to go and find Shikanoko. There are many forces at work and I don't understand them all, but I believe they are converging, with the purpose of restoring the true emperor to the throne."

"People say this terrible drought and the other disasters are all a punishment for the Miboshi's arrogance in choosing the emperor they wanted," Take said.

"You can say such things here in the forest," Hina said, "but never utter them where anyone else can hear you. Your tongue would be ripped out! But certainly in Heaven's eyes there is something grievously wrong. I feel we are being called to set it right. I don't know what to do, except go into the Darkwood in search of your father."

"So my father knows who and where the true emperor is?"

Hina said nothing, not sure how to answer.

Take was frowning as he persisted, "Or is it that you are going to tell him? Are you the only person who knows?"

"Maybe I am, apart from the gods," Hina said quietly. *And Kai*, she thought, but she did not voice this.

AUTHOR'S NOTE

The Tale of Shikanoko was partly inspired by the great medieval warrior tales of Japan: *The Tale of the Heike, The Taiheiki,* the tales of Hōgen and Heiji, the *Jōkyūki,* and *The Tale of the Soga Brothers.* I have borrowed descriptions of weapons and clothes from these and am indebted to their English translators Royall Tyler, Helen Craig McCullough, and Thomas J. Cogan.

I would like to thank in particular Randy Schadel, who read early versions of the novels and made many invaluable suggestions.

All four volumes of Lian Hearn's
The Tale of Shikanoko will be published in 2016.

EMPEROR OF THE EIGHT ISLANDS
April 2016

AUTUMN PRINCESS, DRAGON CHILD
June 2016

LORD OF THE DARKWOOD
August 2016

THE TENGU'S GAME OF GO
September 2016

FSG Originals
www.fsgoriginals.com